A tingling ~~sense of awareness~~ *snapped into place.*

Yep, there she was, crossing the street with her arm linked in a man's. The other man tipped his head to her level and whispered in her ear. Something primal roared to life inside of Cole, reminding him of what was at stake, and it was all he could do to stay seated. Yes, he decided, for Rachel's sake, he would try to play nice....

But at some point, Cole would pony up and meet this guy at the gaming table. Because Cole now knew he was in this for the duration. Somewhere in between seeing Rachel again and remembering how it felt to have her in his arms, he'd made a decision. He was done waiting for the right time, the right words, the right moment or the right anything.

This was war.

Dear Reader,

Like the heroine of this story, Christmas is my most favorite time of year. I am addicted to every one of the trappings the holiday brings—decorations and lights, eggnog and home-baked cookies, shopping and wrapping and, of course, spending time with family and friends.

Christmas tends to bring people closer together. We gather to decorate the tree, bake cookies and exchange gifts. We visit family or welcome guests into our home to celebrate the holiday. And, by and large, people are happier and more upbeat during the Christmas season.

In *Cole's Christmas Wish,* you'll meet Cole Foster and Rachel Merriday. Cole is the youngest of the Colorado Foster brothers, and is determined to show Rachel that they belong together. This would be easier if she hadn't brought a man with her to celebrate the holiday!

So what's a guy to do? Use the holiday and all its trappings to his advantage, of course. Toss in a pretend girlfriend, a nosy-but-well-meaning family, the beauty of Colorado in December and a woman who wants nothing more than to fall completely in love with the *right* man, and how can Cole lose? Maybe this is the Christmas his wish—and Rachel's—will finally come true.

I hope you enjoy Cole and Rachel's story, and I wish you the merriest of Christmases!

Tracy Madison

COLE'S CHRISTMAS WISH

TRACY MADISON

HARLEQUIN®
entertain, enrich, inspire™

Recycling programs
for this product may
not exist in your area.

ISBN-13: 978-0-373-65713-1

COLE'S CHRISTMAS WISH

Books by Tracy Madison

Harlequin Special Edition

*Miracle Under the Mistletoe #2154
*A Match Made by Cupid #2170
*An Officer, a Baby and a Bride #2195
†Cole's Christmas Wish #2231

*The Foster Brothers
†The Colorado Fosters

Other titles by this author available in ebook format.

TRACY MADISON

lives in northwestern Ohio with her husband, four children, one bear-size dog, one loving-but-paranoid pooch
and a couple of snobby cats. Her house is often hectic,
noisy and filled to the brim with laugh-out-loud moments.
Many of these incidents fire up her imagination to create
the interesting, realistic and intrinsically funny characters
that live in her stories. Tracy loves to hear from readers.
You can reach her at tracy@tracymadison.com.

To my agent, Michelle Grajkowski,
and my editor, Gail Chasan.
Thank you both for your support, wisdom and encouragement.

Chapter One

Christmas had all but exploded in Steamboat Springs, Colorado. Wreaths adorned with big red bows and holly berries hung from doors and windows, lampposts and storefronts were strung with sparkling white lights, holiday music played inside and out, and everywhere Cole Foster looked, people—residents and tourists alike— were literally glowing with cheer.

There were a few, he noted, who walked quickly, either because they were used to the frenetic pace of a larger city or because they were intent on reaching their destinations after a full day of shopping, skiing, or both. Still others chugged along the sidewalks slowly, enjoying the sight of Steamboat Springs dressed in its Christmas best.

The locals, on the other hand, fell somewhere in between, neither rushing nor dawdling, yet obviously focused on going home or getting to work. Typically, Cole fell into this group, especially after a long, busy day dealing with the ins and outs of managing the sporting goods store his family owned. Today, however, he wasn't going home.

He stopped and shoved his hands into his coat pockets, breathed in a deep lungful of fresh, cold December air and took a moment to gather his bearings. Thick, fat snowflakes dropped lazily from the sky, enhancing the appearance of the perfect Christmas village. It was, he admitted, a beautiful night.

The weight didn't lift from his shoulders, though. Nor did the anxious adrenaline pummeling through his blood abate. Hell, this year, he had more in common with the Grinch than he did with jolly ole St. Nick—and he had no one to blame but himself.

He'd waited too long to act on his feelings, and while there were reasons for his slow-footed approach—valid reasons, dammit—too long was, at the end of the day, still too long. And now, Rachel Merriday might have gone and fallen in love with someone else.

So yup, the merry had been sucked clean out of Cole's Christmas.

Ironic, really, at the timing. For months, he'd thought about Rachel's visit, about how he was finally going to broach the "taboo" topic and put their past behind them. So maybe, just maybe, they could return to what they were beginning to share before the accident that had changed everything.

Four years ago—had it really been that long?—his entire future looked bright. His career in downhill skiing was speeding along, his relationship with Rachel was starting to turn the corner from the friendship they'd always had to something more—something deeper. One fall—one disastrous fall—had ended not only his career, but the aftereffects had sent Rachel running.

Shouldn't have been a surprise. Rachel's first instinct when anything skewed off-balance was to get the hell out of Dodge. Hadn't he seen her bolt time and time again throughout the years? Yep, he sure as hell had. Just not with him. So when she had, that bit in hard. Real hard.

Unfair, perhaps. He still didn't know exactly why Rachel hadn't stayed, hadn't stuck with him when his world shredded apart. Oh, she'd called. Sent care packages and notes of encouragement, but she hadn't been physically present throughout his year of rehab, or for the time it took to get his head screwed on straight again.

In fact, she hadn't returned to Steamboat Springs until last Christmas, when they'd somehow managed to breach the gap and reestablish their friendship in person. It had been too soon to dredge up the past—their one and only kiss and the words they'd each said the night before the accident—so he'd waited until *this* year. Until *this* Christmas.

Except, a little over a week ago, Rachel had called to inform him that she wasn't coming to Steamboat Springs alone for the holidays. Nope. She was bringing a man with her. A man she deemed might be "the one." Just that fast, all of Cole's plans had disintegrated into dust.

He inhaled another breath and walked on, nodding at and greeting those on his path to the coffee shop. When he arrived at the Beanery, he paused again and glanced inside the windows, in search of a woman with long blond hair and bright blue eyes.

Nope. She wasn't here yet.

Cole pushed open the door and was hit by a blast of heat, the scent of fresh brewed coffee, cinnamon rolls—the Beanery's specialty—and the sound of voices mixed with more freaking Christmas music. What he wouldn't give to hear Mick belting out "Satisfaction" or "Start Me Up," instead of yet another rendition of "Jingle Bells."

A few of the regulars called out to him as he took his place in line. Again, he responded to each with a nod and a smile but didn't initiate further conversation. Rachel would be here soon, and Cole needed every minute between now and then to prepare himself.

The line moved slowly, as Lola—the owner of the Beanery—chatted with each and every customer as if they were her best friend. Beyond the cinnamon rolls, the warmth and camaraderie Lola offered was a large reason why the Beanery was always chock-full of people, even during the few months of the year the town wasn't overrun by tourists.

Usually, Cole enjoyed talking with Lola as much as he enjoyed her cinnamon rolls, but today all he wanted was to get his coffee and escape to an empty table. Preferably one with an unobstructed view of Lincoln Avenue, where he could wait in relative peace for Rachel and "the one," and catch a quick glimpse of them before they saw him.

Body language often told the truth about the state of a couple's relationship. Cole was hoping to see a mile-wide distance that would negate the possibility that "the one"—otherwise known as Andrew Redgrave—might be raring up to propose.

Frankly, the thought made Cole sick to his stomach. Yeah, he'd waited too long to speak his peace, and now—well, now he might lose Rachel before he—*they*—ever really had a chance.

"What will it be today, Cole? Your normal black coffee and a cinnamon roll?" Lola's chipper, somewhat twangy voice interrupted his thoughts. "Or are you in the mood for something fancier for once? Maybe a peppermint mocha or an eggnog latte?"

"Coffee is supposed to taste like coffee, not peppermint or eggnog," he pointed out, taking in the snowmen dangling from her earlobes, the oversize Santa hat pinned to her bottled-red hair and the blinking, multicolored necklace of lights she wore. He grinned. Lola was a character, no doubt about it. "Just the coffee today, I think. Had a late lunch."

Squinting in surprise, Lola grabbed one of the Beanery's bright orange mugs. "Never known you to say no to one of my cinnamon rolls, late lunch or not. You feeling okay?"

"Yup, just not hungry," Cole said quickly. "You know how it is this time of year."

Curiosity lit Lola's gaze, but she nodded and poured his coffee. Cole bit his lip to stop himself from overexplaining. Lola was one of his mother's best friends, and if she suspected anything was amiss, she'd be on the phone to Margaret Foster in the blink of an eye. In another blink, his mother, father, brothers and sister would descend—each determined to discover what the problem was so they could go about rectifying it. Whether Cole wanted their help or not.

"Here you go." Lola slid his coffee across the counter, along with a wrapped-to-go cinnamon roll. "For later, when you're hungry again. My treat."

"Thanks." Arguing, Cole knew, would be pointless. He handed her a few bills to cover the cost of the coffee. "I'll save it for breakfast."

"Your mom was in earlier today," Lola said as she rang up the purchase. "She's ordered several dozen of these for Christmas Eve. I hear you have family coming in for the holidays?"

"Yup. The entire Oregon side of the family, babies included." All three of his Foster cousins were now settled down and, from what his mother had said, blissfully happy. Good for them. "Thanks again, Lola."

After dropping a handful of change into the tip jar, Cole made his way—finally—to a table. Ten minutes, more or less, until he saw Rachel. And Andrew, of course. He couldn't forget about Andrew, though he'd tried his damnedest to do just that.

Rachel had sent him a text when her plane had landed. That had been a little after noon, so she and Andrew had been in Steamboat Springs for about six hours. Her parents weren't in town at the moment, which meant that Rachel and "the one" had spent an entire afternoon ensconced in her family's vacation home. Probably cuddled together in front of a blazing fire with wine and… Cole rubbed his temple and tried to remove the forthcoming image.

He swallowed a gulp of coffee, tuned out the blasted Christmas music and stared out the window. In the time it had taken him to get his coffee, the snow had grown heavier, the light sheen of fluff now covering the streets and sidewalks getting thicker by the minute.

The sight combined with his melancholy state-of-mind took him back in time, to the day he'd first met Rachel. He was eleven, she was ten, and a bunch of the local kids were messing around over at the school playground. Cole and his two older brothers, Reid and Dylan, were involved in one of their massive snowball fights when the mother of all snowballs crashed into the back of Cole's head, sending him sprawling face-first in the snow.

His brothers stood there like statues, their mouths hanging open in shock. Cole pulled himself up with a snowball ready to go, pivoted and saw…her. Pink cheeks, huge sky-blue eyes and short, wispy blond hair that stuck out around her face like a newborn chick's feathers.

A rich kid, based on the fancy boots, coat and car parked behind her. Scowling, Cole lowered his snowball. His family owned businesses that catered to the tourists. Ticking off this girl's parents wouldn't please his folks, and he'd learned that rich-kid tourists didn't take well to being one-upped by the local kids.

It irked him that he couldn't retaliate. Being laid out by a girl wasn't cool, and Reid and Dylan would be merciless in their teasing later. Their sister, Haley, upon hearing the story, would go on and on about how much better girls were than boys, and wow—wouldn't that suck?

Still, he followed his common sense and shrugged it off, as if the dumb girl and her snowball meant less than nothing. His eyes had locked with hers, and she'd given him this spunky, I-win sort of grin that made him even madder, so he turned his back to her.

Seconds later, Cole was kissing the snow again. This time, his brothers broke into laughter. That alone was enough to force Cole into action. Sputtering, he flew to his feet and let his snowball fly. She staggered backward when it smacked her on the chin, but stayed upright. He expected her to stomp her feet and throw a hissy feets, to run to the safety of her car and burst into tears to whomever sat inside.

But she didn't. She smiled broadly, and in almost slow motion, pulled another snowball from behind her back and whipped it through the air, hitting not him, but his brother Dylan square on the chest. That had been the start of their friendship.

For the next many years, Rachel and her parents spent the holidays and the occasional summer in Steamboat Springs, and their friendship grew stronger as they grew older. During their teenage years, they began to stay in touch throughout the months in between her visits, and once they were in college—and after—they found ways to spend time together on a more consistent basis.

Always as friends, though. Until that last year. Until the kiss, the accident and the hell that followed. Cole's gut tightened at the memory. Hell, had he turned into a sixteen-year-old girl? The past was the past, and dwelling on what had happened, versus what might or might not have happened, did him absolutely no good in the present.

A tingling sense of awareness snapped into place. Cole shifted to the right to get a better view and...yep, there she was, crossing the well-lit street with her arm linked in a man's. For a millisecond, he forgot everything else as he watched her long-legged, slender body in motion. Her middle-of-the-back-length blond hair blew around her face, the strands merging with the swirling snow, creating the image of a mythical snow princess.

His heart did the galloping lurch to his throat, and his blood seemed to warm beneath his skin. God, he'd missed her. Even more than he'd realized. He gave himself another few seconds to enjoy the simple pleasure of just seeing Rachel again. She was as beautiful as always.

The man—Andrew—tipped his head to her level and whispered in her ear. Her lips opened in a silent laugh, and she bestowed a light kiss on his cheek. Something primal roared to life inside of Cole, reminding him of what was at stake, and it was all he could do to stay seated.

Narrowing his eyes, he now focused all of his attention on Andrew.

He was tall, but not as tall as Cole. Stupid and meaningless, for sure, but that pleased him. He walked in a smooth, polished gait that spoke of authority, and his black Burberry trench screamed style and wealth. Not a surprise. Rachel came from style and wealth and everything that lifestyle granted, so why wouldn't the man she decreed might be the one?

That didn't bother Cole. What did was how good they looked together. He supposed he could hope there was something wrong with Andrew…some ulterior motive buried behind his interest in Rachel. She'd been involved with men before who were more interested in her family's wealth and her father's business connections than they were in her.

Somehow, though, Cole's intuition told him that wasn't the case here, even though he hadn't yet spoken one word to Andrew. If there was something—anything—going on that could potentially hurt Rachel, Cole would ferret it out. More for her sake than his. Not that he wouldn't use any such information to his advantage, because he would. Without doubt or hesitation.

He supposed he could also hope that Rachel would bolt, as she had with him and other relationships over the years, but wishing for that felt wrong. Cole wanted her to be happy, and that wouldn't happen until she'd figured out that running away never solved a damn thing.

The couple stopped outside the window. Andrew pulled Rachel close for a kiss that reignited Cole's mental images of how they might have spent their afternoon. Cole swallowed, squeezed his hand tight around his coffee cup and waited the interminable seconds until they separated. Rachel said something, laughed again and tugged Andrew toward the door.

It took every bit of willpower that Cole could muster, but he had his smile warm and welcoming when they entered the coffee shop. Rachel squealed, dropped Andrew's hand—which, yeah, also pleased Cole to no end—and flew toward him for a hug.

Standing, he opened his arms and caught her when she landed. Pulled her in tight to him and squeezed. Her scent, a delicious mix of spice and fruit and winter, wrapped around him, securing the knowledge that Rachel belonged in *his* arms.

Soft hair, damp from the snow, brushed his jaw as she whispered, "I'm so happy to see you. It's been too long."

"Good to see you, too," he said. "And it's always too long."

She stepped out of his arms and turned toward Andrew to introduce them. Her pretty blue eyes softened and a glow entered them that Cole had only seen once before—in the seconds before their solitary kiss. Well, hell. So far, nothing was adding up the way he'd hoped.

Widening his smile, as fake as it might be, Cole reached out to shake Andrew's hand. A faint smirk colored Andrew's expression, but he met Cole's hand with his own and—surprising Cole—squeezed a tad harder than required. And then, harder still, as if out to prove his machismo.

Immature, possibly, but Cole wasn't about to ignore the challenge. He tightened his hold incrementally, smiling all the while, knowing he could outlast just about anyone in the handshake wars. It took all of fifteen seconds, maybe twenty, before Andrew gave up and released his grip.

Score one for the home team.

"Good to meet you, *Kyle*," Andrew said as he flexed his fingers. "It's nice to finally put a face to the man that Rachel considers a brother."

"Friend. Best friend," Rachel interjected. "But yes, I made it clear how important *Cole* is to me. And now we're all here! Isn't this wonderful?"

"Wonderful," Cole replied, resisting the childish urge to punch "the one" in the face. He nodded toward the table and retook his seat, saying, "Glad to meet you, too, *Andy*. Up until a week ago, I hadn't heard one word about you, so I'm sure you'll understand my concern… and my questions. Seeing I'm 'like a brother' to Rachel, it's my duty to look out for her welfare."

Andrew scowled but didn't immediately respond. He helped Rachel with her coat before removing his own. Once they were seated, he refocused on Cole. "Oh, I understand," he said with a nuance of sarcasm. "I think this will be fun…getting to know each other. Don't you?"

Rachel glanced at Cole and then at Andrew and then back to Cole, her eyes beseeching him to ease the awkwardness, rather than edging it on.

"Absolutely." Cole lifted his coffee mug in a faux toast, deciding he'd give Andrew one more chance at playing nice. For Rachel's sake.

But if "the one" continued to push at Cole's buttons, he'd pony up and meet him at the gaming table. Even if he didn't, Cole now knew he was in this for the duration. Somewhere in between seeing Rachel and having her in his arms, he'd made a decision. He was done waiting for the right time, the right words, the right moment, or the right anything.

This was war.

* * *

Well, *that* had been a rocky start.

Rachel Merriday leaned back in her seat to wait as Cole and Andrew went to get their coffees. Would they find a way to get along? Certainly, once Andrew realized he had no reason to be envious of Cole, he would relax. Cole, she knew, had simply responded to Andrew's slight antagonistic attitude, and when that ended, would be more than happy to meet him halfway.

Or so she hoped.

The two had a lot in common, not that either one of the stubborn fools would believe that on her say-so alone. While they didn't look alike in any way whatsoever, they were both handsome, virile men. Where Cole was dark—black hair, deep brown eyes and what Rachel described as caramel-coated skin, Andrew was light—ash-blond hair, steely gray eyes and a bordering-on-fair complexion that was more like her own.

Each was tall and fit, but also in different ways. Cole had the look of an athlete, lean and naturally strong. Andrew's slightly more muscular physique came from hours spent in the gym each week and a rigorous low-fat, low-calorie, low-everything diet. But, yes. Both handsome. Both virile. Both sexy as all get-out.

No woman alive could deny that. Or, Rachel amended, no *sane* woman.

The real similarity between them, though, existed beneath their skin. Sure, Andrew tended to be more serious than Cole, but his heart was just as big, just as sincere, just as honorable. They were protectors. Guardians, really, of the people they loved. It was that trait in particular that had first drawn her to Andrew.

Continued to draw her, if she were to be completely honest.

But was she ready to settle down and have babies with him? She didn't know, couldn't quite get there, couldn't yet take the leap from wanting to believing to being. The idea of marrying the wrong person petrified her. The thought of having children in a loveless marriage pushed her into a blacker realm of fear.

She knew all too well what that did to a kid, to the adult that kid became. No. Rachel couldn't—wouldn't—make the same mistakes her parents had. Incessant arguing behind closed doors, portraying the happy, perfect couple—family—at public events, using their child to wage war against the other.

Pretending. Faking it. Smiling when you wanted to cry, scream, stomp your feet, or…yeah, run away. As far and as fast as your legs could carry you.

Even so, as crazy as it sounded, Rachel yearned for love and everything that came with finding the right man. She wanted a family, dammit. She wanted grocery shopping and carpools, fat babies who would become mouthy teenagers, school bake sales and PTA meetings, picnics and backyard barbecues, and she wanted all of that with a man who loved her senseless.

Almost without thought, her eyes landed on Cole, and her heart sort of liquefied and slid to her knees. She'd screwed up there, she knew. And that screw-up had possibly caused her to lose out on something amazing. Maybe even something life-altering.

They were okay now, mostly, she thought. But her regret lived on. And that was why, despite her misgivings, she refused to run away from Andrew. The fear curdling in her belly, keeping her awake at night whenever she considered a future with Andrew, was the same exact fear that had propelled her to run away from her sole regret.

From Cole.

Rachel pushed out a ragged sigh. Her friendship with Cole made more sense than a lost opportunity, and was certainly far more important than a relationship that had never existed. Their friendship was real. Solid. Lasting. That brief flame so long ago? Meaningless.

Of course being here would stir up old memories. One year ago, she'd had all these *possibilities* in her head when Cole had asked her to visit for the holidays. But he'd made it clear—crystal, even—that it was their friendship he valued, had missed. Not the other.

And then Andrew had walked into her life and dazzled her with his charm and sweetness. With the traits that reminded her of Cole, and those that didn't. *He* desired her. *He* talked about making a life together. That was real. That was solid. Was it lasting? Maybe.

That was what this trip was really about. She felt sure she could find a way to be head over heels with Andrew by Christmas, here in her favorite city, with an up-close and personal reminder of what she'd lost due to fear.

All she had to do was relax and stop thinking—analyzing—so much, open her heart and let herself take the tumble. How hard could it be?

Feeling somewhat calmer, Rachel tried to catch the men's attention by gesturing toward the restrooms. Cole noticed, smiled and nodded, and returned to talking with Andrew. She waited for Andrew to glance her way, but he didn't.

He was too focused on Cole, on whatever Cole was saying. Maybe, without her presence, they'd found some common ground. She hoped so. Otherwise, the next few weeks were going to be even tougher than she'd expected. And that... Well, that wouldn't help her cause at all.

Chapter Two

Rachel took her time freshening up, needing a few minutes of privacy to settle her churning emotions. When she returned to the table, the men were waiting silently with rigid shoulders and hard, stony jaws. Okay, so that was a no to them finding some common ground.

She slid into place next to Andrew and wrapped her hand around the whipped-cream, syrup-drizzled cappuccino sitting in front of her. Unsure of how to proceed, she sipped her coffee slowly, her mind thinking of and rejecting possible topics of conversation.

"This is so good," she said, infusing brightness into her tone. "What did you two get?"

"Black coffee," they both said at the same time, in identical flat inflections.

Aha! Common ground. Going with it, Rachel said, "Well, they have great coffee here."

"They do." Cole's lips twitched into an almost grin. "Want me to get you some?"

"But I—"

"Because what you're drinking," Andrew said matter-of-factly, "isn't coffee."

Cole's grin widened a hair. "Nope. What you have there, Rachel, is dessert."

"Wow, like minds and all that." Rachel took another hefty swallow of her "dessert," and said, "Is this one of those 'real men don't eat quiche' sort of things? Or in this case, real men don't drink fancy coffees?"

"Nah. I like quiche." Cole picked up a napkin, leaned across the table and wiped the corner of Rachel's mouth. The touch was quick and effortless, but a flood of warmth overtook her just the same. "A little whipped cream was…er…anyway, it's gone now."

She felt more than saw Andrew stiffen beside her. In another second, his arm was cradled over her shoulders. He tipped her chin toward him and kissed her. Also quick. Also effortless.

"There. *Now* it's all gone." Andrew settled into his prior position, keeping his arm snug around her. "I hope that didn't make you uncomfortable, Kyle. She's just so kissable, I couldn't help myself."

"Not at all," Cole said with a good ole boy grin and a laidback shrug. "Nothing there to feel embarrassed about. Why, I've given my mother the same type of affectionate peck in public on more than one occasion." He winked at Rachel. "My sister, too, now that I think about it."

"Didn't say I was embarrassed." Andrew shifted an inch closer to Rachel. "Some people dislike public displays of affection. I belatedly thought you might be one of them."

"Nope." Again with the shrug. "But I appreciate your concern."

"Wow, is it cold outside!" Rachel blurted before Andrew could respond. She faked a shiver. "So…cold. I still haven't warmed up from the…um…short walk here from the car."

"We could be in Hawaii right now, sipping mai tais by the ocean." Andrew kissed Rachel again, this time on the top of her head. "If you're having second thoughts, we could be on a plane tomorrow. All you have to do is say the word."

Cole's eyes narrowed in annoyance. Rachel understood why. She and Cole had made plans *before* Andrew had asked to join her…which he hadn't done until after Rachel had refused to cancel this visit to go with him to Hawaii.

She guessed Andrew saw that as choosing Cole over him, but that wasn't the case. Not really. Mostly, it was about going home for the holidays. Because in many ways, Steamboat Springs was the closest she'd ever had to a real home.

Due to Cole and his family, though, not hers.

"I'm not having second thoughts, but I like the idea of going to Hawaii for your birthday in May. If you still want to."

"Of course I do." Andrew's voice was smooth. "I simply wanted to give you the option, now that you've seen your friend."

"Thank you, but I'm good. And we'll have fun here!" She patted Andrew's arm. "You'll soon see why I love Steamboat Springs so much, especially at Christmas."

"You've never been here before, Andy?" Cole relaxed in his seat, looking for all the world as a man completely at ease. "Odd, but I swore I recognized you when you walked in. A lot of people come through here every year…thought maybe you'd vacationed with an ex-girlfriend. Or, perhaps, an ex-wife?"

Good grief. If it wasn't one thing, it was another. "Andrew doesn't have any ex-wives."

"And I never will. I don't believe in divorce."

"Who does? I doubt anyone marries believing they'll divorce," Cole said in a conversational, let's-get-to-know-each-other manner. "But divorce happens. Sometimes, folks marry too young, pick the wrong person, make mistakes in the heat of the moment. Sometimes, a relationship becomes so messy that divorce becomes the only option that makes any sense."

He spoke from experience. His brother Dylan was divorced. In his case, they were married too young, she cheated and became pregnant, and ran off with the other guy. So while Rachel didn't believe in divorce, either, she agreed with Cole's take.

Heck, she'd be the first to stand up and cheer if her parents untied the matrimonial knot.

"You're right, but only to a point. A lot of those scenarios can be written off as the result of poor decisions before a proposal is given…or accepted." Andrew clasped her hand tightly in his. "When I put a ring on a woman's finger, it will be forever."

Cole leveled a weighted, questioning stare on Rachel. "Life can often be…unexpected. It's how each person reacts to some of those moments that can make or break a relationship." Pausing, he bent his head ever so slightly toward Andrew, but kept his sinfully dark eyes glued to hers. "You can analyze all you want, think every last thing through, and you still won't know for sure until you're in hip-deep. In my opinion, of course."

The urge to squirm came on strong, but she ignored it. Was he referring to her littered-with-broken-relationships past, or was he sending her some type of a hidden message regarding Andrew? Darn if she knew. For not the first time in Rachel's life, she wished she could read Cole's thoughts.

"Anyway," she said, drawing the word out slowly, "Andrew hasn't been to this part of Colorado before, so I have a lot to show him. I can't wait to take him skiing."

One of Cole's eyebrows shot up. He looked at Andrew. "Is that so? Are you a skier?"

"No, I'm not. But—"

"Snowboarding, then?"

"No," Andrew repeated. "I've skied before, naturally, but my skill level is that of a beginner. But for Rachel, I'm willing to give the sport another try."

Nodding enthusiastically, Cole said, "That's good. Rachel loves to ski…snowboard…ice skate." Pure pleasure gleamed in his voice, in his eyes. "And, going back to your earlier comment, sharing the same interests is important in any successful relationship. Again, in my opinion."

Andrew sat up straighter. "Which is why I'm excited to give the sport another try. As I said."

"Well, what you said," Cole drawled, "was that you were *willing* to try. Not quite the same as excited."

She was, maybe, three seconds away from clobbering them both. Right on top of their manly heads. "There are lots of interests that Andrew and I share. We bike, go to the gym…um…horses! I love horseback riding and Andrew is an excellent horseman. He grew up on a ranch in Texas."

"That's great to hear. Plenty of horseback riding to have here in Colorado. I still think, though—" Cole broke off and scratched his jaw "—I know! How about if we pick a day and hit the bunny slope, Andrew? We can go over the basics, get you up to speed, as it were."

"I can handle a bit more than the bunny slope," Andrew replied in a dry manner. "And frankly, I'd rather have my girlfriend as my teacher. I think of it as one more way for us to grow closer. Which is, after all, an important aspect of this visit."

Cole glanced at Rachel and her frisson of alarm escalated. She knew that expression. It meant trouble with a capital T. Darn it all, what had he latched on to now? She reached toward him, intent on grabbing his arm to divert his attention, but he leaned away before she could get a proper hold. Her fingers skimmed against his skin and the mere touch sent a bolt of heady awareness through her body, startling her with its strength.

"Wow, guys. I'm sorry to hear that. I mean," he said with a slow, methodical beat, "if you need a vacation to grow closer, something must not be going well. Let me know if I can be of any help…anything at all, just say the word."

"Our relationship is fine," Andrew snapped. "If there were problems, I wouldn't assume a vacation could fix them."

"We're absolutely fine!" Rachel said a good deal louder than necessary. Andrew's declaration stung, though. She had, indeed, brought Andrew with her in the hopes the time away, the time together, would erase her reservations. "Just fine."

"Ah, hell. I didn't mean to hit a sore spot." Cole held his hands up, gesturing a truce. "Forget I said anything. I'm sure you guys are…*fine*. Just as you've both said."

Itchy with frustration and nerves, Rachel did the only thing she could think of: she changed the subject. Again. "How's business at the store this year, Cole?"

"Same as always during the winter months" was his quick, humor-ridden, reply. "Lots of folks in and out. Between rentals and new sales, classes, and private lessons, we're doing well."

Andrew tightened his hold on Rachel's shoulder. "That's right. You work for your parents now. I hear you were quite the skier in your day, so I'd imagine the unexpected, even traumatic, change in careers could feel…stifling? Limiting, perhaps?"

Whoa. Rachel pulled out of Andrew's grasp, shocked by his words, his rudeness and his insinuation. He was never like this, never purposely hurtful to anyone. Jealous or not, uncomfortable or not, he'd gone too far.

"You don't understand how the Foster family functions, Andrew," she said. "Cole and his siblings are an integral part of the *family*-owned businesses. They manage, work and own them together. Isn't that right, Cole?"

"That's correct," Cole answered, still appearing more amused than anything else. "But no, Andrew, there isn't anything stifling about the arrangement. I'm grateful to my folks for what their hard work and commitment has provided me and my brothers and sister with."

After a lengthy pause, Andrew combed his fingers through his short hair and sighed. "My comment was uncalled for. I apologize."

"No harm done," Cole said with ease. "My family is exceedingly close. Sometimes, a bit too close, but we are what we are and I wouldn't want anything to change."

"That's important," Andrew said, his voice almost gruff. "My family…isn't as close. You're a lucky man."

In a heartbeat, Rachel forgave Andrew for his jab. Something had happened to put distance between him and his family. She didn't know the details, but she knew he missed them.

"I am lucky," Cole agreed. "In many ways."

"I consider myself fortunate, as well, for finding Rachel." Andrew exhaled a breath, and when he spoke again, she heard the man she'd been dating for the past few months instead of the stranger he'd become upon meeting Cole. "Are you seeing anyone special, Cole?"

Every one of Rachel's knotted muscles relaxed. The posturing was finally over, thank goodness and hallelujah. Maybe now, the two men would find some true common ground.

She waited for Cole to answer Andrew's question, but when he didn't, she did for him, saying, "Nope. Cole isn't dating anyone."

After all, Cole would've told her if he'd met someone. He always had in the past. And in truth, Cole rarely dated. It was something she used to tease him about, way back when.

A prickle of apprehension appeared at the nape of her neck a millisecond before Cole said, "Actually, Rach... I've been meaning to tell you—" He paused, locked his vision with hers and thrummed his fingers against the table. The rat-a-tat-tat beat mimicked the pounding of her heart. "There is someone in my life. Someone special."

No way. She must have heard him wrong. "You're seeing someone? Someone...special? Really?"

One by one, each muscle in her body tensed again as she waited, as she tried to come to grips with the possibility that Cole was involved in a serious relationship. With someone special, someone important.

Someone who wasn't her.

"Yes," he said firmly, still looking directly, almost intensely, at her. "There is an important woman in my life. She might even be—no, she definitely is—the one for me."

"Okay." Rachel swallowed and tried to push past the nausea that had crawled into her throat. Why did this bother her so much? They were friends. She'd accepted that and had moved on. She shouldn't care. At all. "Well, that's…great news! Why didn't you tell me before?"

Of course, she hadn't mentioned Andrew until a week ago, so who was she to throw stones? Relationships were private. Cole was a private man. He had the right to keep anything to himself for as long as he chose. Solid logic, but his secrecy bugged her. A lot.

Cole shrugged. "You're hearing about her now, and—" Andrew's cell phone buzzed, stopping Cole short.

"I need to take this," Andrew said after glancing at the display. He stood. "Excuse me for a minute."

She watched Andrew step away from the table. Refocusing on Cole, she said, "Go on. What's her name? And what do you mean she's the one for you? When… um, when did you meet her?"

"None of that's important right now." Cole angled his body toward her, so they were eye to eye, and clasped Rachel's hands in his. The heat of his touch didn't come close to thawing her sudden chill. "I'm a goner, Rachel. I've fallen in love and there's no looking back."

"You're joking, right?"

"What do you think?"

Rachel stared into the eyes she knew so well. Eyes she'd seen filled with almost every emotion in the book. And now, she saw something intense and passionate lurking in the depths, along with a desperation that made *her* heart ache. In other words, she saw love.

Every instinct she had wanted to deny what she saw,

but she couldn't. "I think I have to meet the woman who finally captured Cole Foster's heart," Rachel whispered in shock. "I never thought…never…" She blinked. "Well, isn't this terrific? I'm so happy for you."

Leaning in closer, Cole plopped a friendly—*brotherly*—kiss on her cheek before easing away again. "You're with Andrew and think he might be the one. I've fallen in love with someone I *know* is the one. I have a hunch," he said with a wink, "that this Christmas will be *very* memorable."

"Right. Memorable." That was one description.

"You look a little pale, Rach. Are you feeling okay?"

"Oh, yes! I'm just…tired." She gulped another large mouthful of coffee. "You know how traveling is."

"I do."

She tried to think of something, anything, to say to fill the gap, but couldn't. Cole was in love. That was fine! Of course it was. She had Andrew, for crying out loud. "Um. Andrew should be back any minute," she mumbled. "That was probably a business call."

"Business on vacation, huh? He must be dedicated."

"He is. He… I know he wasn't on his best behavior at first," she said, suddenly finding it very important to build up Andrew. For her sake or for Cole's, she didn't know. Even so. "But he really is a great guy."

"I'm sure he is," Cole agreed.

"Just…give him a chance before deciding you don't like him. That's all I ask."

"I can do that. He took me off guard with that Kyle crap, but it's obvious he cares a lot about you. The fact he does, and makes no bones about it, goes a long way for me."

"So…are you saying you approve?"

"You don't need my approval, Rach," Cole said quietly. "You know that, right?"

Rachel shook her head, still trying to clear cobwebs. "Yeah. Of course I do."

Cole beamed a smile. "Just like I don't need yours."

"Right. No approval necessary." She sucked in a breath, taking the air in so deep it almost hurt. "But I'd like to meet your…girlfriend. I mean, if she's going to be a part of your life…"

"I'd like that, too. Unfortunately, Cupcake—that's what I call her—is a little shy. Might take some time, convincing her to agree to an introduction." Pausing, Cole closed his eyes as if thinking something through. "Maybe if it were just you at that first meeting, that would be okay. Less…intimidating than introducing her to you and Andrew at the same time."

"Sure," she said without thought. Cupcake? He called her *Cupcake?* Cole didn't do terms of endearment. Or he never had before. "Andrew can stay at the house."

"He won't mind?" The concerned pretense from earlier returned. "Gee, I don't know about that. I'd hate to cause problems while you're trying to…repair your relationship."

"We're fine, we're not—" Screw it. Let him think what he wanted. Besides, he wasn't wholly off base, even if Andrew hadn't yet arrived at that realization. "That isn't an issue."

"I'd also hate to upset him by taking up too much of your time," Cole said in complete and utter sincerity. "From what I gathered, Andrew appears to have a jealous nature."

"Now that Andrew is aware you're in love with another woman," Rachel said, nearly choking on the admittance, on the reality of the situation, "I expect the jealousy to fade."

Cole hesitated, as if mulling over the idea. Finally, he nodded. "Well, then, I'll set something up. Just try to keep your schedule open. Convincing my Cupcake to step out of her shell won't be all that easy. And while she isn't impatient, exactly, once she makes her mind up about something, she can be rather determined."

"What is she? Shy or bossy?" Rachel said the words that popped into her head, even though she probably shouldn't have. "Because by your definition, she's both, and honestly, I haven't met very many people who fall into both categories."

"Let's call her...complicated. That's a good word to describe this particular woman."

"Complicated?" She snapped her mouth shut and silently counted to ten. Cole jumping through hoops to please some shy, determined, *complicated* woman didn't sound encouraging. It was annoying. And the image, the very thought of it, rubbed Rachel in all the wrong ways. "I already don't like this woman," she muttered.

"What's that? I couldn't quite hear you."

Gripping her coffee cup so hard that her knuckles ached, Rachel forced her mouth to move into a smile. "I said that I can't wait to meet this woman."

"I knew you'd be excited for me." Cole reached over to tug a lock of Rachel's hair, just as she'd seen him do a thousand times to his sister, Haley. "Thank you for being such a wonderful friend."

"Forever friends," she said, using their childhood phrase. As the words left her lips, the last bit of hope—hope she hadn't known still existed until that second—fizzled out.

Suddenly, she sort of wished she'd chosen Hawaii.

* * *

An hour later, Cole watched Andrew and Rachel leave
the coffee shop, unsure of what, exactly, had propelled
him to create a pretend girlfriend. The touching had irritated him, though he didn't have the right to be irritated. Andrew's posturing had, surprisingly, been more
amusing than infuriating. Well, except for the comment
about Cole's career.

Even so, he hadn't reacted to the push—Rachel had
done that for him—and Andrew's apology had seemed
sincere. At that point, the tension emanating from Andrew had lessened, and Cole saw a glimmer of the real
man Rachel had brought with her to Steamboat Springs.
And damn if he didn't begin to like him...just a little.

Cole certainly had no intention of making up a
woman—a special woman, no less—when Andrew
had then asked about his relationship status. But Rachel
stepped in, answered in the negative, and that—yep, that
was what had done it—had compelled Cole to lie. She'd
been so sure, so damn positive in her response, that Cole
had wanted to shake her up and prove that she didn't
know every microscopic detail about him or his life.

The maneuver had worked, too. If Cole was a bet-
ting man, he'd have wagered cold, hard cash that she'd
turned green with envy over his declaration.

If she was in love with another man, why would she
care if Cole was seeing someone? She wouldn't. Or, he
corrected, she *shouldn't*. By the way her skin had paled
a good two shades and her stunned expression, not to
mention the wobbly state of her voice, Cole had to believe she did, indeed, care. He couldn't deny his satisfaction over that.

But he'd lied, and that bothered him. So now he had
to decide what to do about the fabrication. Confess the

truth or keep the pretense in play? Hell. Lying didn't
sit well with him, but Rachel's reaction, especially her
whispered statement, "I already don't like this woman,"
egged him on, teasing him with the possibilities of what
both could mean.

Cole stood, waved goodbye to Lola and headed out
into the December night, thinking through those possibilities. What he'd said wasn't a complete untruth: there
was a special woman in his life. A woman he loved, a
woman he saw himself quite capable of spending the
rest of his days with, having children with, growing old
with and every last thing that entailed.

Rachel, of course.

A plan, crystal clear in its clarity, formed in Cole's
mind. He could use his real feelings for Rachel, along
with what she believed to be true, and enlist her help
in wooing "the woman of his dreams." If Rachel was
jealous, if she did hold more than friendship for him in
her heart, wouldn't that be enough to propel her to act?
Maybe.

Or it could backfire. Send her scurrying even deeper
into Andrew's arms, into a future with him, and—like
she'd done before—away from Cole. But hell, what did
he have to lose?

If he did nothing, he'd gain nothing.

The snow still fell as he walked toward the sports
store, where his truck was parked on the street out front,
and a magical—dare he say, *Christmassy*—feeling wove
in and wiped out his inner Grinch. He had to try. Had
to see if he could resurrect the flame between them.

And if he couldn't? If Rachel loved Andrew, if *he*
made her happy, then nothing Cole did would change
that. But maybe, if luck was with him, the process would

allow him to put the past to rest. So he could move on and get Rachel out of his head.

Once and for all.

Chapter Three

Rachel finished loading the dishwasher with the break-fast dishes and faced Andrew, who had just returned to the kitchen after taking a phone call. "What do you want to do today? The snow's falling a little too thick for skiing, but we could walk around the town, take in the sights, look for a tree...do some Christmas shopping. Whatever you want."

"I'm sorry, Rachel, but that was the office," Andrew said, gesturing toward his cell. "There are some issues with a potential client that will likely require my attention."

"Oh." Rachel fought off her disappointment. Andrew owned a management consulting firm, and she was already well-versed in the putting-plans-on-hold department. He was busy, traveled extensively and rarely made it through a meal, let alone an entire day, without an interruption. "Well, you warned me this would be a working vacation. Is it serious?"

"Maybe. Too soon to tell yet, but we should probably—"

"Stay in today," Rachel finished his sentence for him. "That's fine! We can dig out the Christmas decorations, so they're ready to go when we find a tree, watch some old movies, play a board game." An idea occurred to her. A nice, homey, tradition-filled idea. "Hey! Feel like baking some sugar cutouts?"

"You're amazing, do you know that?" Approaching her, Andrew dropped his phone on the counter and pulled her into a hug. "You've never given me grief over my job, over the demands placed on our relationship because of it. I appreciate that in you, Rachel."

"I'm glad you've noticed," she joked, standing up on her tiptoes to brush her lips over his cheek. "Because sometimes, your job is a pain in the butt."

"I know it seems that way, especially since your schedule is typically so clear," he said, referring to Rachel's careerless life. "But the company is in a crucial period right now. We're growing fast, which is good, but I have to ascertain we're able to sustain the growth, see to our existing client base, bring new clients on board, all while expanding and training staff."

His comment burned, a little, even though she knew he hadn't meant any harm. She kept herself busy enough with her parents' social events, where her attendance was deemed mandatory, charitable causes and their functions—of which, there were plenty, and the odd class here and there, when something pulled at her interest.

But Andrew was right. Her schedule was infinitely clearer than his.

"I understand all of that, Andrew, which is why I

don't give you grief." She appreciated his appreciation, but she'd enjoy his undivided attention a bit more. Especially now, on their first full day in Steamboat Springs. "So…what will it be? Cookies, decorations, games or a movie?"

"Cookies sound—" Andrew jerked to grab his phone, but it wasn't his cell buzzing. It was Rachel's "—delicious. Go ahead and get that. I'll search the cupboards for ingredients."

Nodding, Rachel answered without looking at the display.

"Hey there, Rach. How's your morning treating you?" Cole asked, jovial as all get-out.

The sound of his voice—the rich, deep ring of it—sank in like butter melting on a hot, fresh-off-the-griddle pancake. That, along with his upbeat mood, caused her attitude to dip another degree. Still, she kept her tone chipper when she said, "Wonderful. How's yours?"

"Good. Real good, in fact." Someone said something on his end that she couldn't quite catch, but she heard enough to know the speaker was female. Was it her? The complicated, shy-yet-determined Cupcake? "Haley says hi," Cole said. "And wants to know if you have any clothes you're angling to give away."

Haley. Cole's sister, not his girlfriend.

Rachel laughed, in relief and in humor. Last year, when Haley had stopped by for a visit, she'd raided Rachel's closet, oohing and ahing at the designer labels. She'd been so excited, Rachel had given her a boxful of outfits: dresses, shirts, pants and a couple of jackets.

Rachel didn't need them. Her mother shopped to show her love…and she shopped a lot. Which, Rachel supposed, said something. "Tell Haley to stop by whenever," she said. "My closet is her closet."

Cole relayed the information. Haley squealed and jabbered something else. Rachel smiled even broader. She adored Cole's family. For a long while, when she was younger, she'd pretend they were her family. *Her* parents, her brothers, her sister.

Well, except for Cole. She'd never thought of him as her brother.

"Believe it or not, the reason for my call has nothing to do with my sister's fetish for clothes," Cole said, returning his attention to Rachel. "If you're available—and I'll understand if you're not, seeing this is last minute— I thought we could meet up for lunch."

"Lunch? Today?" Andrew, she saw, had found the flour and sugar. She pointed toward the cupboard that held the mixing bowls. "As in, you and I? Or will your significant other be joining us?" No way, no how would she resort to calling a stranger "Cupcake."

"I believe she will be present, yes."

"Really? That fast? I thought you said it would take some time to convince her to meet me. Since she's so shy and all. Or did I misunderstand you?"

"What can I say? Women are a mystery. Just when I think I have one figured out, they veer off course and I have to start from scratch." Exhaling a short, noisy sigh, Cole continued, "I gotta say, Rachel, you females are a confusing lot. Say one thing when you mean another. Speak in code half the damn time, and usually, we poor men are left in the dark."

"Uh-huh. You 'poor men' rule the world, rarely call a girl when you say you're going to, and usually, leave us poor women wondering what we did wrong to elicit such behavior…and scrambling to figure out what we can do to fix it."

"Sweetheart," Cole said in that drawling way of his,

"the perception might be that men rule the world, but the facts are that women rule the men. Your team has the upper hand in every negotiation with my team. Ask Andrew if you don't believe me."

"I'll do that." Huh. If that were the case, then why did Rachel forever feel as if she were on the losing team?

"Later. But only if you ask your sister."

"Deal. I'll be interested in hearing his take," Cole said with a chuckle. "About lunch?"

"Well…" Rachel stalled, unsure if *she* was prepared to meet Cole's Cupcake just yet. "Andrew and I are baking cookies and we might…um…bake a lot. So not really sure if today—"

"Go, Rachel," Andrew said, pausing his search of her cupboards. "I'll probably be tied up soon enough with work, anyway. I'm sure we can get at least one batch of cookies baked first."

"One sec," she said to Cole. Then, covering the phone with her hand, said to Andrew, "Are you sure? I don't know how long I'll be gone."

"Lunch with Cole *and* his girlfriend, right?"

"Yes."

"Then I'm sure." He opened a drawer and discovered the measuring spoons. "You can get out of the house for a bit and I can focus on my job without feeling guilty. Seems like a win-win situation. On all accounts."

"Right. Win-win." Discouraged and, not that she'd admit it, somewhat annoyed, Rachel nodded and put the phone next to her ear. "Lunch is fine, Cole. When and where? Foster's?" she asked, referring to the family-owned restaurant and pub. Where else would they go?

"No," Cole said after the briefest of pauses. "Let's go to Dee's Deli. Say one o'clock?"

"Um. Sure. I'll see you then." Hanging up, Rachel

smiled absently at Andrew, who was now organizing the items he'd placed on the counter. It was cute. And… homey. "All set."

"Good. Are you excited to meet Cole's better half?"

"I'm more interested than excited. As far as her being his better half? I'd say that remains to be seen." Her irrational irritation at the whole mess broke free with, "He calls her Cupcake. Cupcake! Isn't that ridiculous? She isn't a toy poodle, for crying out loud."

"Perhaps she resembles a toy poodle, hence the nickname?"

"What?" Rachel tried to picture that possibility and came up blank. "You mean if she's petite and has curly hair? Or…I don't know, Andrew. How can a woman resemble a poodle?"

"I was joking, Rachel." Andrew looked at her curiously, the concern in his gray eyes evident. "It's a term of endearment. Why are you upset? Does it matter what he calls her?"

"I'm not upset…I'm—" She stopped, sighed. "No, it doesn't matter in the slightest. I guess I'm used to these visits going a certain way, and this time, everything is different."

"I see." Andrew crossed the distance between them and kissed her on her forehead. "Forget about Cole and his Cupcake. We have cookies to bake," he said with a grin. "I haven't made Christmas cutouts since I was a child. Maybe this is the start of a tradition for us."

"That's a sweet thought…and a nice one."

"I like it, too. I'm sorry about work butting in today," he said, his voice and his expression earnest. "And for my attitude with Cole last night at the Beanery. Forgive me?"

"Of course," she murmured. "Nothing to forgive."

Pivoting, unable to handle his scrutiny or his sweetness, she located the cookie cutters and dumped them on the counter before grabbing the cookbook. "Let's make a tradition."

Andrew's gaze still held concern, but he didn't push the topic. Just nodded and joined her at the counter. Rachel tried—oh, how she tried—to stay in the present, to enjoy this time with Andrew, but her mind kept traveling down other paths.

Yes, darn it, what Cole called his girlfriend mattered. Why hadn't he mentioned her real name? And really, using only a term of endearment when talking *about* someone else was odd. Also, and even more telling, Rachel mused as she measured flour into the mixing bowl, was that he'd suggested Dee's over the family restaurant.

Maybe Cole's family didn't approve of the relationship? Oh, wow. That would mean…

Anxiety pooled in Rachel's stomach and pinpoints of pain jabbed at her temples. If so…then yes, Cole truly loved this woman. His family and their opinions were too important, too valuable to him to remain involved with a woman he didn't have real feelings for.

"Darling?" Andrew's amused tenor broke into Rachel's thoughts. "I think you went a tad overboard on the flour. We're not opening up a bakery, are we?"

Rachel stared into the mixing bowl, now almost filled-to-the-brim with flour. About, she guessed, four times the amount necessary.

"I'm sorry," she whispered, not sure if she meant her mistake or the fact she'd been thinking about another man when she should be focused on Andrew. On finding her own slice of happiness. "I…don't know what happened."

"Hey, don't worry about it." Andrew started scooping flour back into the storage container. "See? Easy enough problem to fix."

Right. Easy as pie. Too bad she couldn't say the same about cupcakes.

Well…one particular cupcake. Rachel sighed and attempted to push what didn't concern her out of her mind. Her goal should be to surround herself with the present, with Andrew. If she were very fortunate, perhaps she'd soon be taking a leap of her own.

Into Andrew's arms.

Cole stood outside of Dee's Deli with a to-go box in his hands, waiting for Rachel to arrive. It might be a little—or by some folks' perspectives, a lot—cold for a picnic, but he'd heard Rachel's surprise at the fact he'd chosen Dee's over Foster's for lunch.

He couldn't take her there until he'd had a chance to talk to his family. His convoluted plan would go up in flames the second Rachel asked any one of them about his girlfriend. In the light of day, he wasn't so sure he could pull this off anyway, but he knew he couldn't if his family refused to get on board. Tonight, Cole decided, he'd see what they had to say.

Until then, he figured a winter picnic would suffice well enough as an explanation for that particular decision. Explaining why his Cupcake was absent from the picnic was another story, but he thought he could deal with that little issue on the fly. Hoped so, anyway.

Thankfully, the snow had lightened considerably in the past hour, and Haley had readily agreed to watch over the store solo for the afternoon. Mostly because he'd asked her to do so last year during Rachel's visit, so in her mind, this wasn't any different.

For the next five minutes, Cole went over his plan and

the words he intended to use. A tight rope, for sure, portraying a man in love with a made-up woman to the real woman he was actually in love with. There were holes in his plan. Big, gaping holes that he hadn't quite worked out how to fill. If he played his part too strong, Rachel—assuming she still had feelings for him—might keep those feelings to herself, in the name of his happiness.

Conversely, if Cole didn't play the part with enough realism, she—again, assuming she even had those feelings—might not be propelled to unbury them, or, hell, to even recognize they existed. Cole's goal, therefore, was to strive for a balance.

Of course, determining where the line was between "too far" and "not enough" could prove problematic. He'd have to play it by ear, be ready to make adjustments at a second's notice and hope he achieved the right balance at the right time.

He'd given some thought to just telling Rachel what his feelings were, which had been his original plan before he'd learned about Andrew. Now, after going down that road for all of thirty seconds, Cole had dismissed it outright. The humiliating truth of the matter was that he didn't think he could take being shot down while another man was in the picture.

This way, at the very least, he retained some control. Some dignity. If Rachel didn't bite, he'd have his answer soon enough without handing her his heart to decimate. Later, after she'd returned to New York, he'd simply tell her his relationship with Cupcake had come to an end.

No harm. No foul.

Their friendship would live on, Rachel would never know the truth, and Cole would continue living and working in Steamboat Springs. Someday, he might even meet another woman that he'd be able to envision a future with.

He caught sight of Rachel crossing the street, barely skirting the pile of snow left by the curb as she stepped off of it. She was, he realized, stuck deep in her head somewhere, thinking of who knew what and not paying attention to her surroundings.

In that moment, with his vision centered on Rachel, *someday* seemed an impossibility. As if the reality of loving another woman—*any* other woman—existed in a different world. One very far from the world Cole—and Rachel—lived in.

Right before she'd left the house, Andrew had sequestered himself in her father's office with his laptop and phone. The cookies were baked and cooling, ready for frosting when Rachel returned. Andrew had promised that if all went well on his end, they could see about getting a tree that evening. If all did not go well, they could go tomorrow, or the next day.

They had plenty of time. Almost two weeks until Christmas day, so another day or two or three shouldn't make a difference. But it did.

She'd put off her lack of Christmas spirit to the fact she hadn't yet immersed herself in the season. Christmas had always been her favorite holiday, her most favorite time of year, and she wanted to reclaim the happy glow that usually came so effortlessly.

To her, that meant choosing the perfect tree posthaste.

The tree was the visual epicenter of the holiday. You wrapped gifts to put under the tree. You sat around the tree to look at the lights, maybe even to sing a few Christmas carols. You hung ornaments from Christmases past on the tree's branches to recall the memories and emotions you experienced one year ago, two, three...and more.

Everything surrounded the tree. Sure, she could find one on her own. She'd done so before. But to further her goal of falling head over heels for Andrew, she wanted to do so with him. Create more traditions, as it were. First, though, he needed to clear his schedule, so he could enjoy himself and not stress over business-related problems.

Honestly, she had to wonder if it would have made more sense for Andrew to have stayed in the city until a few days before Christmas. She knew he hated dealing with work issues from afar, so she guessed he'd prefer to be in New York now, rather than here with her.

That is a pessimistic attitude, her inner voice chided, *and you have no idea if that's how Andrew feels.* True. But she couldn't help the way *she* felt.

Plus, frankly, coming to grips with her nonsensical irritation, shock and other various emotions regarding Cole's relationship would be easier if she didn't have to worry about what Andrew was doing, or how he felt, or...

Lost in thought as she was, she didn't see Cole until she'd just about barged into him. One arm reached out to steady her, stopping her from slipping on the snow-slicked sidewalk. She gasped, righted herself and took a purposeful step backward.

Flustered, she pulled in a breath. "Didn't see you standing there."

"I noticed." Dark brown eyes simmered in amusement and something else Rachel couldn't name. "Have to be more careful or one of these days, you're going to run into a wall."

Been there, done that. What she said, though, was, "Thanks for the warning."

"That's me, always willing to lend some helpful advice," he said, deadpan. "Are you okay?"

"I'm fine." *Calm down,* Rachel instructed herself and her out-of-control pulse. This was Cole. Her friend. Her *good* friend. "What are you doing out here instead of inside?"

"Waiting for you."

Rachel arched an eyebrow. "Again. Why out here?" Oh. Maybe he had something to tell her, something he couldn't—or wouldn't—say in front of his girlfriend? "Is there a problem?"

"Nope. Not a one." Grinning, Cole held up a to-go box. "Thought we'd eat outside today, is all. Cupcake enjoys winter picnics and I like to do things that make her happy."

"Isn't that…nice." Rachel loved the outdoors, but really—a picnic in the dead of winter?

"She thinks so." His expression became contemplative. "If the thought isn't appealing to you, I'm sure Cupcake will understand. She doesn't have a lot of free time today, though, so we'll probably have to put this meeting off to some other—"

"No!" Ouch. Way too loud. Lowering the volume, Rachel said, "I love winter picnics, Cole!" She looked around, didn't see anyone resembling a toy poodle. Or for that matter, an actual toy poodle. "I assume she's meeting us there…wherever *there* is?"

"Good assumption. I've always appreciated your above average observational skills."

"Are you being sarcastic?"

Instead of replying, he winked and curved his free arm through hers. "We should get a move on," he said.

"Before you freeze standing there. The walk will help warm you up."

"I'm warm enough, but sure…let's go," Rachel said brightly. "We wouldn't want to keep her waiting."

"Nope," Cole agreed as they took off at a brisk pace. "That would be rude."

"And she wouldn't like having to wait, would she?" Ugh. She hadn't meant to sound snide. "Based on what you said last night, that is, about her being *determined* once she makes up her mind."

"Why, Rachel Merriday, are you calling my girlfriend impatient?" Cole's body shook with silent laughter.

"Yes, actually," she said, his amusement pushing her irritation to new heights. "I am."

He let out a heavy-sounding sigh. "I'll admit that her tendency skews toward the impatient side, but I find the trait rather endearing. Helps keep me on my toes."

"You've always preached patience," Rachel pointed out, disliking the mysterious Cupcake more by the second. "To me, anyway."

"Yup, I have. You two are quite a bit alike in the impatience…*determined* department." Cole guided her around a small group of folks gathered in front of the hardware store. "In a manner of speaking, our friendship has gone a long way in preparing me for this relationship."

Rachel stopped and narrowed her eyes. "Are you implying that I'm a complicated woman, Cole Foster? Because if you are—"

One long, weighty look halted her words. Goose bumps popped up on her skin and a tremble passed over her as he, inch by inch, appraised the full length of her body.

"Wh-what are you doing?" she stammered.

"Ascertaining you're still a female," he said. "And you are. So yes, Rachel, you're a complicated woman. As is my sister, my mother and every other woman I've ever known."

Unable to regain her bearing, Rachel started walking again, though she had no clue where they were headed. Over her shoulder, she said, "I guess that means you owe me."

He caught up to her, his long stride erasing the distance she'd created in no time flat. "Owe you for what?"

"Why, preparing you for this relationship, of course." With a flip of her hair, she marched forward, refusing to look at him again so soon after her body had darn near melted.

Once again, he entwined his arm with hers. He slowed their pace down to that of a leisurely stroll. In a voice dripping with laughter, he said, "Oh, you have, and you're right, I absolutely owe you. What's your price?"

"We can start with 'Cupcake's' first name," Rachel said as they approached the local elementary school. Hmm. If they were having lunch here, did that mean Cole's girlfriend was a teacher? "It's becoming tiresome referring to her as a baked confection…or the generic 'her' or 'she.' So what gives, Cole? What's her name?"

"Driving you crazy that you don't know, isn't it? There," Cole said, nodding toward and then leading them in the direction of the school playground. "I'll brush the snow off one of the benches and we can get settled."

"Cole!" Rachel said, exasperated, and okay, a little crazy. "What. Is. Her. Name?"

"Uh-huh, driving you crazy. I bet," he said slowly, "you're coming up with all these excuses why I haven't told you yet. One of them is probably that my family doesn't approve."

"Do they?"

"They like her just fine, Rachel." He shrugged, causing a lock of black hair to fall on his forehead. Her fingers itched with the want to stroke it back into place. "But I can't tell you her name."

"You...*can't* tell me your girlfriend's name?" Rachel yanked her arm out of Cole's and settled her hands on her hips. "Why in the world wouldn't you be able to give me such basic information about the woman you're seeing?"

"Why do you do that?" he asked instead of answering. "Repeat my statement in question form, as if ascertaining you heard me correctly? You know me well enough, or you should, to know I don't say something unless I mean it."

"Because what you're saying is absurd."

"Only because you don't have the proper information." Cole handed her the box of food. "Give me a minute here, and I'll explain everything. Over lunch."

It was a Thursday, but the playground was empty. Too cold and snowy for outdoor recess, apparently. Rachel shielded her eyes and turned in a circle, looking for the woman they were supposed to be meeting. No sign of Cupcake. Shouldn't she be here by now?

"She isn't here," Rachel said, giving heed to the instinct she'd had ever since Cole's phone call that morning. "She isn't coming. She was *never* coming. Isn't that right, Cole?"

Cole faced her, his expression serious. "No, she isn't. I used meeting her as an excuse to give us some privacy, without Andrew's presence."

"I see." Rachel counted to ten, slowly. "Why?"

"Because I need your help."

"My help? What type of help?"

"See? You're doing it again, making a question out of my statement."

She tapped her foot once. Twice. And waited.

"It's like this, Rachel." He placed his hands on her shoulders and looked her straight in the eye. "My mind is set on proposing to this woman I love, on Christmas day. But I'm experiencing some…let's call them difficulties, in getting her to see our relationship the way I do. I need your help in romancing her, priming her, so to speak, so she'll say yes."

"Proposing? As in…marriage?" Rachel whispered, not caring in the least that she'd rephrased his statement as a question. "As in, *this* Christmas?"

"That's my goal. And that's why I can't, or won't, tell you her name. I want someone who doesn't have any preconceived notions about…Cupcake." He paused, as if weighing his words. The corners of his mouth curved into a tiny grin. "Yep, that's what I need. Someone who can be *objective* in their advice, based on what *I* see in this woman, in what *I* tell them."

Rachel swallowed, backed out of his hold. "And you're afraid that if I know her name, I'll…what? Somehow learn something about her that will hinder my ability to…help you *woo* her? By the simple virtue of having her name?"

"Exactly! Why, you might accidentally bump into her at the Beanery, or at Foster's. If you don't know her name, you won't know it's *her,* see what I'm getting at? Or you might hear some folks chatting, and if her name came up, you'd be all over that." His smile widened in smug satisfaction, as if he were extraordinarily pleased with his explanation. "This way, you have to rely on the information I give you, so your viewpoint will be the same as mine."

"I see."

"I knew you would." Cole grabbed Rachel's hand and squeezed tight. "This woman is special. Every detail needs to be right. *Just* right. She deserves so much more than she knows, and I want to be the one to give her everything. And more."

Wow. Just…wow.

"I guess I don't understand," Rachel somehow managed to say. "If you love her, and she loves you, why do you need any help? Especially mine?"

Turning away, Cole brushed the snow off the bench and gestured for her to sit. She didn't. Just kept her mouth shut and waited for him to answer her question.

"She's had…some problems with a few of her past relationships. And a rocky childhood, I guess you'd say. She has all these barriers because of both." Cole shifted his gaze away from hers. "I'm afraid if I'm not careful, she'll bolt. I can't let that happen, Rach."

"Oh." His logic clicked solidly into place with a sickening thud. A tremble passed through her, and then another, before she found the courage to voice the obvious. "Her past sounds a lot like my past, doesn't it, Cole?"

He nodded.

"So from your perspective, we're both impatient, complicated women who share similar issues." Moisture appeared behind Rachel's eyes, threatening tears. She blinked them away. Fast. "That's why you want my help in particular, correct? Because you think I'll somehow have an inside track into how to get around these specific barriers?"

"That and the fact you're my best friend."

"Right. Best friend." Well, at least he was honest. The throbbing in her temples returned. "I… This is a surprise."

Cole watched her with a speculative gleam. The tense set of his shoulders, his jaw, his very stance declared how important this was to him. "I don't need an answer right now," he said. "I know I'm asking a lot, especially since this could potentially steal time you'd planned on having with Andrew. Ask whatever you want, take however long you need."

Closing her eyes, Rachel tried to rationalize a way she could gracefully decline. She could use the Andrew excuse he'd just given her, but honestly, based on the happenings that morning, she felt fairly sure the majority of Andrew's vacation would be claimed by work.

She could just say no. Simply state the prospect made her uncomfortable. Oh, God. This was…unthinkable. Her chest tightened with pressure and her throat closed. She so didn't want to do this, didn't want to help Cole—a man she'd once hoped would be *her* man—romance another woman into marrying him.

So, yes, she could say no. *Should* say no. But she'd left him once before when he'd needed her. Had taken off due to fear and complications and a host of other issues she'd never fully explained. Issues she still didn't completely understand herself. She'd hurt him. Heck, she'd hurt *them*…not only what might have been, but their friendship.

No. She wouldn't do that again. Despite how difficult this might be, she couldn't turn her back on his plea. In that second, in no more than a single beat of her heart, Rachel gave in and accepted her fate. Fully, this time. Cole Foster and Rachel Merriday were friends. Forever friends.

"Okay, then." Opening her eyes, she infused cheery and merry into her tone with all of her might. "Let's see what we can do about getting you engaged. We'll call it—" she paused, took in a gulp of air to center herself "—my Christmas present to you."

He came to her then, hugged her so hard that she lost the rest of her breath. "Thank you," he whispered, the warmth of his body easing into hers. "I couldn't do this without you."

Merry freaking Christmas, indeed.

Chapter Four

The second Cole returned to work that afternoon, he phoned his mother. With Rachel's agreement in place, bringing his family into the picture became even more crucial. Fortunately, getting the entire Foster clan together on short notice hadn't proved difficult. One small hint regarding his current personal dilemma had sufficed.

In no time at all, his mother had arranged a late dinner at Foster's Pub and Grill, set for after the evening rush had ended. When Margaret Foster summoned her family, they came. No questions asked. Short of a local or national emergency, anyway.

Dinner had progressed smoothly enough, as Cole had kept the conversation firmly in the casual zone. Once the plates had been cleared and dessert served, unable to ignore the questioning glances from his mother and father any longer, he cleared his throat and dived in.

"So," he said, "Rachel's in town. She arrived yesterday."

"Is that so?" Margaret asked with a small smile. "And how is Rachel?"

"Good. She's…good." Dang. This was going to be harder than he'd thought. "She brought a man with her. His name is Andrew and—" Cole cleared his throat again. "She mentioned that he might be thinking of proposing. I'm…ah…not too keen on that idea, actually."

"Is that so?" his mom said again. "Why would that be?"

Five pairs of eyes regarded him curiously. A few of the gazes held amusement, as if they already knew Cole's answer. Hell. Maybe they did.

"She barely knows him, for one thing."

"Uh-huh. Any other reason?"

He was going to have to say it. He'd known that coming in, but that didn't make the prospect any easier to choke down. "I'm in love with her," he half growled. "That's why."

No one spoke for all of ten seconds. Then, "Is that so?" asked Cole's father, Paul, repeating his wife's words in an amused tone. "Can't say that's headlining news, son. We've known your feelings for Rachel for quite a while."

Cole shook his head in mild exasperation, not really surprised. When had he ever been able to keep anything from his family? Not very often, and never for very long. "Well, in that case, maybe the rest of this will go easier."

"The rest of what?" asked Reid, the eldest sibling. He, Cole knew, would be the hardest to convince. Reid followed the rules, all of them, whether the rules made a lick of sense or not.

"The rest of what I have to tell you." At this point,

Cole paused and sized up his family. He figured his best shot resided in Haley. His sister was a romantic, so convincing her shouldn't be overly difficult. Even better, getting her on board would be a two-for-one deal, as Dylan—the middle brother—tended to side with Haley in most matters.

This was important. For decisions that required the entire family's input, the Fosters followed the majority-vote-wins concept. Haley plus Dylan plus Cole was half of the battle won. Then, he'd only need to pull over his mother or father. It would likely be his mother, but with Paul Foster, you never could say for sure.

"It's like this," Cole said, focusing on Haley. "I believe that Rachel might have…similar feelings for me. I can't let her marry another man without finding out if I'm right. But Rachel is stubborn and…well, to counteract that, I did something. And now I need help to see it through."

Cole continued on, explaining what had occurred at the Beanery, and then earlier that day at the picnic. Haley's mouth softened into a gooey smile the longer he talked, which was a positive sign, while Reid's hardened into an uncompromising frown, which wasn't. Though, Cole hadn't expected anything else from his never-color-outside-of-the-lines big brother.

What he didn't say, or even broach upon, was his lingering concerns over Rachel's ability to commit, or his back-and-forth thoughts and feelings regarding her departure after his accident. Neither topic was up for public debate. They were issues for he and Rachel alone to discuss.

And they would, one way or another. Doing so was an integral part of his plan, just as important as discerning her feelings and determining if they could have the fu-

ture he envisioned. But he had to proceed slowly, carefully. And he had to start somewhere.

Not one member of his family interrupted him as he
spoke. He supposed they were balancing his words with
what they knew about him, about Rachel. By the time
he finished, his throat felt parched and heat had gathered on the back of his neck. He loved his family. He'd
relied on them throughout the worst moments of his life.
He trusted them.

But damn if this didn't feel as if he'd just stripped
naked in front of them. Difficult, yes. Also, though,
humbling and far too revealing for his peace of his mind.

"That's everything," Cole said to break the silence.
Rather than their earlier amusement, his family now appeared disconcerted—if not downright shocked—by all
he'd had to say. Well, that was fair. He'd dodged their
questions regarding Rachel for years, and now, seemingly out of the blue, he'd made his feelings plain *and*
had asked for their help. In one fell swoop, even.

"Let me ascertain I understand you," said Cole's father, his expression stern and serious. "You love Rachel,
Rachel is here with another man, she now believes you're
in love with a local gal, and along with all of that, you've
elicited Rachel's agreement to assist you in convincing
this other woman—a woman who doesn't exist, I might
add—into accepting a marriage proposal?" He paused,
drew in a breath. "Is that about right?"

When his dad looked at him in just that way, Cole felt
about five years old. Still, he managed to keep his voice
calm and collected when he said, "Yes. That's right."

"Okay, then." Paul's steady brown eyes never left
Cole's. "That's quite the plan you've arrived at here.
It's creative, if nothing else." He paused again, as if

considering the dilemma. "I'm assuming you've already thought through other possibilities?"

"Well, of course he has, Paul," Margaret Foster inserted. "Cole never does anything without thinking every possible option through. You know that as well as I do."

"Now, Margaret, our son is asking us to lie to a woman we all like," his dad said in that patient, authoritative way of his. "I think a few questions are in order before we agree."

"I am not in favor of lying to anyone, particularly to Rachel," Reid said, his words clipped and distinct. "Really, what were you thinking? You want to have a relationship with this woman, right? Why would you head down that path by misleading her?"

"Oh, stop. We don't have to lie to Rachel." Haley wrinkled her nose at Reid. "Weren't you listening? She isn't supposed to ask about the girlfriend, and even if she does, all we have to say is, 'No comment. Cole asked us not to discuss this subject.' Which he did. So, no lies necessary. Geez, pay attention."

"Avoiding the truth is still a lie, Haley," Reid said, as set in his ways as ever. "You adore Rachel, consider her a friend, and you're okay with deceiving her? You truly don't see a problem with doing so?"

"Rachel *is* my friend," Haley said quietly but with conviction. "And if the end result is my friend and my brother being happy together, then yes, I'm okay with this. I've always thought they'd make a terrific couple." Narrowing her eyes, Haley pointed at Reid. "You have, too, for that matter. You've said so! Stop being such a...a...stick in the mud."

"Yes," Reid said drily, "being an honest person equates to being a stick in the mud." Giving up on their sister, Reid shoved his fingers through his short, cropped hair and aimed his gaze at Cole. "You're playing with fire. Even if this initially pans out how you hope, what will happen when Rachel discovers the truth? Have you considered that?"

"Yup," Cole said, striving for an easy, nonchalant tone. Not so simple when he held the same concerns his brother had just expressed. "I have, and I don't know, and you're right. But the plan is in motion. It seems to be working. The best I can do is keep moving forward. But I need your help." He swung his gaze around the table, including his entire family. "I need everyone's help. I wouldn't ask if this wasn't important to me."

"I get that it's important," Reid said stubbornly. "But there has to be a better solution."

"There isn't. Not at this juncture," Cole said, just as stubbornly. The two brothers stared at each other in silence for a few seconds, neither willing to give in. It was, Cole reflected, almost the same as staring into a mirror. All of the Foster siblings resembled each other, but Cole and Reid looked the most alike, sharing the same coal-black hair and deep brown eyes.

Conversely, Haley and Dylan had their mother's warm brown hair—complete with reddish highlights, which Dylan hated—and sage-green eyes. While their mother had a petite, curvaceous figure and tended to work hard to keep the pounds off, all four siblings had taken after their father in that respect, having tall, lean frames and a kick-butt metabolism.

"There is always a better solution." The muscle in Reid's cheek twitched, clearly stating how annoyed he was by the entire prospect. "You just haven't thought of it yet."

"Maybe you're right, but I'm going with this," Cole

said. "I won't let anything get out of hand, and I won't hurt her. Trust me in that regard, at least."

"I do trust you. And I know you would never purposely hurt anyone, let alone Rachel." Reid pushed out an exasperated breath. "I'm also concerned about *you* getting hurt. You've gone through enough, and I just don't see how this can possibly end well."

"It might not," Cole admitted. Pressure descended on his shoulders, reminding him once again of everything that was at stake. The truth was, though, "I'm willing to risk the possibility."

Suddenly, even though he hadn't expected to get Reid's approval, he wanted it. And though he knew better, though he knew that bringing up the one and only woman Reid had ever loved was hitting below the belt, he couldn't seem to stop himself once the idea took hold.

"What if a simple 'avoidance of the truth' had kept Daisy in Steamboat Springs?" Cole asked, hating himself for poking at this wound. "You two would be married now, would probably have children. Can you honestly sit there and tell me that you wouldn't have gone the exact same route as I'm suggesting if it would have made a difference?"

"Cole!" their mother said loudly. "What happened with Reid and Daisy is between them, and has nothing to do with you and Rachel, or why we're here tonight."

"It's a fair question." The cords in Reid's neck tightened, but his voice was firm and even. Controlled. "An 'avoidance of the truth' is exactly what sent Daisy running on our wedding day. So, to answer—yes, Cole, I can sit here and tell you that I would not follow the path you're suggesting. Under *any* circumstance. I already know where it leads."

Whoa. As far as Cole knew, Daisy had simply gotten cold feet at the last moment. Obviously, there was more to the story. Curiosity and concern for his brother rose up, but he squashed it down. If Reid hadn't shared the details before, then it was unlikely he would now. Later, though, Cole promised himself, he'd dig in and see what information he could find.

"I'm sorry," he said instead. "I shouldn't have brought Daisy into this."

Reid gave a stiff nod, but didn't say anything else. Lost in the past, Cole presumed. A past that Cole shouldn't have tried to use to his advantage. Great. Some brother he was.

Dylan, who up until now had remained quiet, said, "This is getting us nowhere. It's a simple matter, really. Cole never asks for our help. Ever. He has, and that alone is enough to sway me." He shrugged. "For what it's worth, I'm in."

"I feel the same." Haley pushed her chair closer to Reid and rested her head on his shoulder. "But if Reid is that uncomfortable with this, then maybe we—"

"No. Don't worry about me. It's…it's fine," Reid interjected in the same controlled, even manner as before. At everyone's look of surprise, he grinned halfheartedly. "Dylan's right. Cole never asks for anything from any of us. I'll go along and hope—" he tugged on their sister's hair "—for a positive result. Besides which, someone needs to get on grandbaby duty before Mom starts arranging our marriages."

"Why, I would never—" Margaret broke off as everyone burst into laughter. She sighed. "Grandbabies would be nice. Seeing my children happy and settled would be nicer. And from a woman's perspective, I find Cole's idea holds a touch of romance, which appeals to me. So, with that said, and with Reid, Haley and Dylan's agreements, I'll do my part." She squeezed her husband's arm. "What do you say, Paul?"

The patriarch of the family gave his wife a sidelong glance. "I have to echo Reid's earlier statement—beginning a relationship with subterfuge is risky. However—"

"Now, Paul—"

"However," Cole's father continued, "a man is apt to crush the sides of the box when he falls in love, if he thinks it will help. I certainly did. My goal will be to stay clear of Rachel until this mess is over with, but if I were to run into her—I'll play along. Just don't take this too far out of bounds, Cole. Emotions are involved. Not only yours, but Rachel's."

"I won't and I know." That was one thing he didn't need reminding of. Cole swallowed past the lump that had manifested in his throat. He had just received something that rarely occurred within the Foster ranks: a unanimous vote. "Thank you."

The words were meant for everyone, but he looked at Reid as he spoke them. Learning that his by-the-book brother had skirted outside the rules once and, if Cole were to follow the path of logic, had lost Daisy as a result had stunned him. It also helped him understand Reid a bit more than before, gave him some insight into what made him tick.

"You're welcome," Reid said. "Just…be cautious."

Cole nodded for his brother's benefit. He'd be a fool if he didn't give credence to Reid's earlier comments, to the potential danger of ruining any chance of a future with Rachel due to this charade. Hell. If he really screwed up, he could lose her friendship, as well.

A rush of nausea twisted in his stomach and a wave of light-headedness made his vision swim. Rachel not being a part of his life in any way at all was an inconceivable thought. On the outside, his brother's advice was solid and in line with Cole's earlier decision. Somehow, though, in the course of this conversation, something had changed. Now, he didn't think being too cautious was going to take him where he wanted to go. Too much action could, as he had already surmised, send Rachel running.

Yet another fine line to balance upon.

"It seems," he said to no one in particular, "that having a pretend girlfriend is going to prove more troublesome than having a real girlfriend ever has."

Dylan snorted. "Real or pretend, all girlfriends are trouble. I'll take the pretend one any day of the week."

"Amen to that," Reid said, leaning over to smack Dylan's palm in a high five. "Or in my case, the no-girlfriend route."

"I miss being a girlfriend," Haley said wistfully, tucking a chunk of reddish-brown hair behind one ear. "And I want a real man in my life, not a pretend one." She scowled at each of her brothers. "It's your fault I'm single. You've scared every interested man off, all three of you."

"I thought you had a date tomorrow night? With that nice young man that manages the bookstore?" their mother asked. "Has something changed?"

"What man?" Reid said.

"Do I know this guy?" Dylan asked.

"See?" Haley groaned and proceeded to explain that who she dated wasn't anyone's business but her own.

From there, the conversation turned completely away from Cole. He listened as his brothers teased Haley, joined in here and there, but mostly stayed in his own head, thinking about Rachel. They were meeting tomorrow, to shop for "Cupcake," to go along with the romancing-the-pretend-girlfriend plan he'd outlined over lunch.

One gift a day—preferably a gift of a romantic, personal nature—leading up to Christmas, which was when, he'd explained to Rachel, he'd get down on one knee and propose. The gifts, of course, would all relate to Rachel in some form or fashion. To *their* relationship.

He appreciated the irony that Rachel would have a hand in choosing the gifts based on what Cole told her about his "girlfriend," when, in fact, every description would be about Rachel. Would she catch on? Probably not. Most people didn't, or couldn't, see themselves as others did. But she might.

Rachel was an intelligent woman, after all. She could very well recognize herself in Cole's words, confront him, and then—after hearing him out—give him a sweet, pitying smile, a hug, and say, "I'm flattered, Cole, but I love Andrew. I thought you knew that."

Cole grimaced and tried to put the God-awful thought out of his head. Because, frankly, being kicked in the balls sounded a hell of a lot more appealing. Not to mention, infinitely less painful. And yeah, that pretty much said it all, didn't it?

"Wait a minute. You're coming here? For Christmas?" Rachel said into her cell from her parked car on early Friday afternoon. No, no, no. The last thing she needed was her mother's special brand of craziness for the holidays. Especially now. "I thought you were staying with Dad, because of some important Christmas party he insisted you attend. What changed?"

"Everything," Candace Merriday said, her voice cool and unrelenting. "I am no longer interested in giving *that man* anything he wants or insists upon. Not after what he's done."

"Hmm," Rachel said, ignoring the opening. When she was a child, she loved watching repeats of the old television program *Lost in Space*. Now, quite clearly, she heard the Robot's voice in her head, saying, "Danger! Danger, Rachel Merriday."

She didn't need the warning. Asking any questions, showing even the minutest amount of curiosity or interest or concern, would put her smack in the middle of the battlefield. Or, as Cole used to say, she'd become the tennis ball her parents lobbied back and forth, each swing harder than the last, until the ball split apart.

Not a pretty picture, but somehow, despite her best efforts to remove herself from the equation, she almost always became the tennis ball. Right now, though, she didn't have the strength or the time to deal with her parents' latest crisis. She was meeting Cole in less than ten minutes, and she wasn't sure she'd be able to muster the strength for that.

Her mother heaved a long, drawn-out, dramatic sigh. "Are you there, Rachel Marie?"

"Yes, Mom. Still here."

"I thought I lost you. The connection between our phones tends to be spotty."

Well, no. Their connection was fine. What she referred to were the frequent gaps in conversation whenever they were on the phone. Rachel stayed quiet, let her mother do most of the talking and only responded when necessary.

It was easier that way.

"Are you definitely coming here for Christmas?" she asked, because securing that information fell into the necessary-for-Rachel's-well-being range. "And if so, have you booked your flight yet?"

"I am, but no. Not yet. Today, probably. Or tomorrow. There's…a lot to take care of. I'll email you the details." The sound of high heels clacking speedily against the floor clued Rachel in to the state of her mother's emotions. She never paced unless she was really, really upset. Ladies don't pace, they glide. "Have you talked to your father today? Or last night, maybe?"

"Neither. Haven't heard a peep from him."

"You've checked your email?"

"Yep, about an hour ago. No emails, phone calls or texts from Dad," Rachel said, biting back a sigh of her own. "Which is basically what 'haven't heard a peep from him' means."

Silence. Candace Merriday did not appreciate sarcasm from anyone, but most especially not from her daughter.

"Sorry, Mom. I shouldn't have said that. I'm in a hurry, though, and—"

"Aren't you interested in what your father did to upset me?" Candace asked. "Or are we to the point that you don't care in the slightest what happens between your parents?"

"I… Of course I care. It's just that I'm…" Rachel trailed off while she thought of an appropriate lie. She did care, but no, she couldn't claim she was interested any longer. That boat had sailed years ago. "I'm driving. The roads are a little slick. Sorry if—"

"Why didn't you say so? We'll save this conversation for when I'm there, face-to-face." The clicking stopped, signifying that the pacing had, as well. For now, anyway. "But do let me know if your father contacts you. You will, won't you?"

"Mom, I really think you and Dad should handle this dilemma without me. So if he contacts me, I'll wish him Merry Christmas and leave it at that."

More silence. A heavy, weighted silence begging for a very specific response.

Surrendering, Rachel said, "But yes, if he calls or emails or texts, I'll let you know."

"That would be good. So," Candace said as her heels started clacking again, "I'll talk to you soon, my darling. Drive safe. Kisses!"

The call, thankfully, ended. Rachel stared hard at her phone, almost expecting her father to choose that second to contact her. When a full minute ticked by without him doing so, she breathed a sigh of relief and powered down the phone. She'd have enough on her mind for the rest of the afternoon without any additional interruptions from her forever-feuding folks.

She loved them. She even enjoyed spending time with them in small doses, without the company of the other, but the continuous tug-of-war had taken its toll. Some people, Rachel reflected as she stepped from her car and headed toward the sporting goods store where she was meeting Cole, should never have gotten married in the first place.

Her parents definitely fell into that category.

They obviously weren't happy, hadn't been for as far back as Rachel could recall. So why didn't they give up the charade and get divorced? Perhaps it was time to ask. She'd certainly have ample opportunity soon enough, seeing as her mother would be here within days. A week, max. Most likely, her father would follow—important Christmas party or not.

Because despite the continuous upheaval in their relationship, Lawrence and Candace Merriday never stayed apart for very long. If one ran, the other followed. Every freaking time.

God. It would be an all-out war. A bubble of desperate laughter choked out of Rachel's constricted throat. Between the prospect of that and her ridiculous promise to Cole, she honestly wished she was spending the holidays anywhere other than Steamboat Springs, Colorado.

New York. Hawaii. A third-world country. A freaking iceberg in the middle of nowhere. Heck, at this point, she'd be happy any place that her parents weren't and she didn't have to listen to Cole wax poetic about a woman he called Cupcake.

Unexpected warmth trickled along her skin. *Cole.* She lifted her chin, and her eyes found him instantly. Again, he stood outside, waiting for her. Like always, he looked tall and strong, solid and...yeah, sexy. He also looked, Rachel admitted to herself, incredibly, unbelievably happy. Well, why wouldn't he be happy? He was in love.

She forced her lips into a smile, raised her hand in a wave and continued to march forward, even though all she wanted to do was climb back in her car and run for the hills.

Where she could hide until she found a way to deal.

Chapter Five

Instead of fighting the crowds at the mall, Cole had decided to stick with the small, local shops that dotted the streets of Steamboat Springs. It was, perhaps, a somewhat dangerous choice. The merest mention of his "girlfriend" to a friend—or heck, an acquaintance—they might bump into could, depending on said friend or acquaintance's reaction, burst his plan into smithereens in three seconds flat.

But come on, how romantic could a shopping mall possibly be? Not very. Alternatively, the picturesque beauty surrounding them, the quaint stores and everything else that attracted tourists to his hometown held charm and appeal and yes, to Cole's frame of mind, the perfect romantic setting. Okay, maybe perfect was a bit of a stretch, but it beat the mall in spades.

"How do you want to do this?" Rachel asked in a clipped, all-about-business way. It seemed she was taking her agreement to help very seriously. Cole couldn't quite decide if that was good or bad. "Talk as we roam or grab a coffee first, come up with a few ideas and then tackle them one at a time? Actually," she said with a sharp, decisive nod, "let's go that route. We'll get everything done faster."

"Nah. Where's the fun in that?" Speeding the process along was not on his agenda. His hope was to spend the entire afternoon with her, not just a few hours. "I like the roaming and talking idea. And," he said with a grin, "I was thinking I could help you, too."

Rachel arched an eyebrow. "With what?"

"Your Christmas shopping, of course. I know you're not done yet," he teased. "You always wait until the last minute. Your mom's love of shopping did not rub off on you."

She gave a faint shrug. "True enough, but I'm not ready to shop. My tree isn't up yet."

"And you can't shop until you have a place to put the gifts, right? Well, we can take care of that today, too."

Shaking her head, she said, "Can't. Promised Andrew we'd do that together. Maybe tonight. Or tomorrow. Or... Well, it will be soon."

Disappointment hovered in her voice, and that bugged Cole. He was well aware of how much Rachel loved Christmas, and therefore, everything that came with—including decorating.

"Hey," he said, "don't look so glum. If Andrew doesn't find the time to pick out a tree in the next day or two, I'm sure he'll understand if you and I do so. As you said, he's a good guy, and good guys prefer their girlfriends to be happy. Right?"

"Right."

"Then let's focus on shopping." He rubbed his hands together. "It will be fun, I promise."

"Uh-huh. Fun. Why, I've been looking forward to this all day." She did that blink-blink-pause-blink thing of hers and her eyebrow arched a smidgen higher.

"Me, too. Glad we're on the same page," he said with equal sarcasm.

"Are you ill? Or…I don't know, delusional? You hate shopping as much as I do."

"Typically," he agreed, taking her by the hand. "But this is *special* shopping, and it's Christmas, and therefore, I'm looking forward to it."

"Uh-huh. Definitely ill." She smiled, but it looked forced. One way or another, he'd get a real smile out of her before the day's end. Firming her shoulders, as if readying herself for battle, she said, "Well, then, Mr. Christmas Spirit, let's get going. It's freezing out here."

He came this-close to teasing her about the various methods he could use to warm her up, but kept the words to himself. Unfortunately, ridding the mental images of those methods proved substantially more difficult. So, for the moment, he settled for a nod. They started down the sidewalk in companionable silence, hand in hand. It felt…natural. Easy.

The way it *should* be.

Excepting, of course, for the pretend girlfriend they were supposedly shopping for and the very real man waiting at home for Rachel.

"What's Andrew up to today?" Cole asked, feeling guilty he hadn't before. "He's okay with all of this, isn't he?"

"Andrew is working. Apparently, he's the only person at his company capable of handling any and all issues that arise, the second they arise." She stopped and shook her head. "That wasn't fair. Andrew told me in advance that this would be a working vacation. And yes, he is fine with our arrangement. Even said he's relieved that I have 'something to occupy' my time while he's busy fixing the latest crisis."

"Ah. I take it you were right, then, about his jealousy fading?"

"It would seem so."

"Well, I suppose that's good news."

"I suppose so. It's just…irritating after the way he behaved toward you at the Beanery."

"Irritating as in you would prefer for Andrew to remain jealous of our relationship?"

She tugged his hand and began walking again. "Yes. No. I mean, not our relationship specifically, but the fact I'm spending an entire day with a handsome, sexy man. That *should* bother him on some level. Shouldn't it?"

"You think I'm handsome? And sexy?"

She looked at him and rolled her eyes. "As if that's a surprise to you. Do you not remember the fan-girls who used to slip their panties into your pockets at bars? Or the ones who knocked on your hotel doors wearing nothing but a coat? Yes, you're handsome."

"Hey, the panties thing only happened once."

"Three times. It happened here, once in Vail and once in Aspen. That's three."

Hell. Her memory was better than his. "The hotel thing, that only happened…never mind." Without even trying, he could recall a half dozen or so instances, so he shut up on that topic. Though, he couldn't resist adding, "You didn't say sexy that time. Only handsome."

She mumbled something about men and their egos under her breath. "Yes, sexy, too. Geez. Happy now?"

"Extremely. Mostly, though, I'm glad you're not get-

ting friction from Andrew." They'd reached the corner
of the street. He gestured toward a gift store that carried
handcrafted items made by local artists. "This looks as
good a place to start as any," he said, leading her inside.

The bell on the door jangled when they entered and
Christmas music—naturally—met their ears. While the
store was not overly busy, there were a handful of customers milling about, none of whom Cole recognized.
Yep, definitely a good place to start.

"I love this store," Rachel said as she faced him. Her
cheeks were pink from the cold, her lips a delicious ruby-
red that damn near begged to be kissed, and the wind
had tousled her hair so that the strands fell in a wispy
disarray of gold. *Beautiful.*

So beautiful that the very look of her blocked every
last thing out of his head. This, he realized, was just
how she'd appear after sex. Rumpled and... His groin
instantly tightened and his earlier images returned, further clouding his ability to think, speak or...hell, breathe.

"Is she an artist?" Rachel asked curiously.

"Ah...is who an artist?" If he took one minuscule step
toward her, he'd be within kissing distance. The want—
no, the *need*—to do just that became overpowering. He
almost gave in to it, almost took that step and claimed
her mouth with his. But his mind chose that second to
replay her question, logic kicked in, and he remembered
what they were doing here, in a gift store.

Even more to the point, he figured out who she was
asking about. The girlfriend...his *Cupcake.* God help
him. "No. She isn't an artist," he said somewhat abruptly.

"A collector, then?"

"Nope."

Rachel swung her gaze around the smallish space,
giving Cole a minute to shift gears. Mentally and physi-

cally. Using a focusing technique from his professional skiing days, he slowed his breathing, relaxed his muscles and envisioned himself achieving his goal as if doing so was a concrete fact, as if failing was an impossibility.

Back then, his goals had been all about winning, about achieving success for himself and for his team. Now, of course, a future with Rachel took center stage. He saw it. Saw *them* as a couple, living their life together, supporting and loving one another.

By the time Rachel returned her attention to him, he was back in control.

"Is there something in particular we came in here for?" she asked, seemingly unaware of Cole's inner struggle. "Or…?"

"No, Rach." That, at least, was an honest reply. "Nothing in particular. We haven't looked at anything yet. The plan was to roam and talk and make decisions as we go, remember?"

"Right." She pushed out a short breath. "Do you have any ideas—even one—of items you might want to give her? So I have something to base my advice on?"

"Nope," he said again, in a purposefully cheerful manner. "Not a one. I'm sorry, Rachel. This could… Well, it could take all day. Gosh, at this rate, maybe all evening, too."

She chewed her bottom lip. In frustration, if Cole had to guess. And yeah, right or wrong, that little action tickled him. It showed that he was getting to her, in some form or fashion.

"Is there anything she needs?" Rachel prodded. "Something you've noticed she could use when you're at her place? Or has she mentioned needing or wanting anything specific?"

"Hmm." He pretended to give the questions some

thought. Then, "Actually, she could really use a new vacuum cleaner. But," he said, mimicking her earlier action and glancing around the store, "this probably isn't the place to find one. Maybe we should hit up Walmart?"

Groaning loudly, Rachel yanked her hand from his. "You're an idiot," she said with a real, true, beautiful-as-a-sunrise sort of grin, "thinking something *that* practical is romantic."

"You asked if she needed anything," he replied with a straight face, once again enjoying himself. "She does. A vacuum cleaner. How does that make me an idiot?"

"I didn't mean something quite so cold and utilitarian!" She crossed her arms in front of her and stared at him. "I meant something...softer, I guess. Like candles or—" Rachel jerked her chin toward a display of quilts "—something pretty and feminine."

He scratched his jaw as if the entire idea confused him. "So I shouldn't buy her a vacuum cleaner, even though she really, really needs one?"

"I suppose that depends on if you want her to marry you or clean your house."

"What if," he said with a wide smile and a wink, "I want both?"

That earned him a smack on the arm. "Idiot," she repeated. "I would suggest you don't include that information in your proposal. If you're aiming for a yes, that is."

"See? I knew you'd have great advice. This is good stuff. Exactly what I need." Because he couldn't resist, he took that step and gave her that kiss. On her forehead, though. "Help me, Rach. I'm out of my league here."

"I said I would help, didn't I?" She bit her lip again. "But I need a name—any name that isn't Cupcake—to call her. Make something up. Like Hortense or...Ingrid."

"Sure," he said, stifling a laugh. Hortense or Ingrid, huh? "What about Bambi? Or…hmm…Jezebel? Cocoa?"

"No. Something *normal*. Something that doesn't sound like a hooker or…or a poodle."

"You have your animals mixed up. Bambi is a deer, not a poodle," he said laughing. "But okay. Let's see…a normal, non-prostitute, non-poodle name." He considered using Rachel's middle name, but figured that would be too obvious. Instead, he went with the first portion of her surname. Merriday. Mary. Perfect. "Let's go with Mary, since, well, this is all for Christmas. Is that normal enough for you?"

"Fine. Wonderful choice." Blink, blink. Pause and blink. "Describe *Mary* to me, please."

"Mary is… Well, she's the most beautiful woman I've ever known." He moved a few feet away from Rachel and feigned interest in the shelf nearest to him, one that held a myriad of pottery bowls, vases and the like. "Inside and out. Her smile lights up a room."

"Well, I guess candles aren't necessary, then," Rachel muttered, making Cole grin all that much harder. Luckily, she couldn't see his face. "I should've asked about her hobbies. What does Mary like to do? In addition to lighting up rooms, that is."

"I wouldn't say she *likes* lighting up rooms. She just smiles and the room glows a little brighter. She probably isn't even aware of how her smile affects me." He selected a short, squat vase that had delicate flowers painted along the bottom. The sky-blue color was a perfect match to Rachel's eyes. "This is pretty, don't you think?" he asked, turning around.

"Beautiful." She tapped her foot. "Great choice. One gift down and you've yet to tell me anything specific about…Mary."

"Who said anything about buying this for Mary? I thought of you when I saw it. The flowers remind me of your eyes." Whoa. He hadn't meant to share that, the words had simply slipped out. Faking a scowl, he returned the vase to the shelf. "Great. Here I had the perfect Christmas gift for you, and you went and ruined it."

"Really? You thought of me?"

"Really."

A slight, wobbly breath whispered out of her lungs. She came forward and bent slightly at the knees, apparently to get a better look at the vase. Grabbing it, she stood straight and held the vase close to her chest. "You're right, the vase is pretty. I'm sorry for…ruining your gift to me, but I have to have it now. So I'll buy it."

Now, her eyes were a breathtaking combination of smoke and pure blue ocean. Still beautiful. Still Rachel. Just a sultrier version of the woman he loved. "Here," he said gruffly, pulling the vase from her deathlike grip. "I'll buy it for you. Since… Well, because I want to."

He figured she'd argue. Women did that a lot, argued when there was no reason to put up a fuss. She didn't, though. Rather, her lower lip trembled in emotion and those unforgettable eyes of hers darkened yet another degree, to a shade reminiscent of the midnight sky.

Blue, but just barely.

"I would like that very much," she said. "Thank you, Cole."

"You're welcome, Rach."

Later, when they were leaving the store with only the vase in tow, she slipped *her* hand in his. Something she hadn't done on her own since…well, since before.

She'd hug him, sure. She'd accept his hand when he reached for hers, absolutely. But this…reaching for him on her own accord was something new. Something different. Something…hopeful.

It was enough. For now.

One gift. After two-and-half hours of "roaming and talking," they'd managed to purchase a solitary present for the woman now known as Mary. Why Cole had seemed so delighted by the snow globe was beyond Rachel's understanding. But he'd honed in on the darn thing as if it were made of gold and coated in diamonds.

The globe was cute, she supposed. It consisted of three separate globes, each depicting a separate scene, put together in the form of a snowman. The scene in the bottom globe was that of a group of kids playing in the snow, sledding, snowball fights and the like. In the middle globe, a pond with more kids ice-skating took center stage, while the top globe—the snowman's face, as it were—showed Santa in his sleigh, flying through a snowy, star-filled night.

So yes, cute. But romantic? Not in Rachel's mind, and she'd told Cole so. Twice. He'd ignored her and bought the overpriced tchotchke anyway, which made her wonder why he'd asked for her advice in the first place. But he had and she'd agreed, so whether he listened to her or not was out of her control. She was good and stuck.

"How many gifts did you say you needed?" she asked. They were at Foster's, which was packed with people, grabbing a quick dinner before heading out to do more shopping. Her mother would be in heaven. Ha. That was a thought. If Cole still required help when Candace Merriday—shopper extraordinaire—arrived in town, *she* could step in.

"How many more days until Christmas?" Cole asked from across the table. He did the math before Rachel could respond. "Not counting today, we have…ten days left, right? So minus the snowman that makes…nine." A pained expression crossed his face. "Ouch."

"Yeah, my sentiments exactly."

"Well, I have the snowman to give her tomorrow. It would be good to find at least one more tonight, so I'm one ahead."

"Let's aim for four more tonight, the final five tomorrow, and call the job done. Otherwise—" she lowered her voice, going for a menacing growl "—I'm turning you over to my mom when she gets here."

Cole winced as her arrow hit home, causing her to grin. She'd brought him up to speed on her mother's phone call and impending visit earlier, somewhere in between store number two and store number three. Both of which were nothing but a foggy haze at this point.

"Um. No. You agreed to help, and I'm holding you to that." Cole lifted his mug of beer and took a swig. "But maybe it's time to have that discussion you mentioned earlier. See if we can nail down a few ideas before heading out again."

"Wow. I'm…shocked." Following his lead, she swallowed a mouthful of her beer before saying, "Finally, you're taking some of my advice."

"Don't tell me you're still bugged I bought the snowman?"

"It isn't romantic! You specifically said you wanted my help in *romancing* Mary. Unless Mary is a ten-year-old girl, and if so buddy, we have other issues to deal with, a toy is not romantic."

"For one, a snow globe isn't a toy. It's a…um…decorative item."

"It's a toy that camouflages itself as a decorative item."

"For two," he said as if she hadn't interrupted, "there are memories attached to that particular snow globe that *are* romantic. We met while—" He broke off and shook his head, clamped his lips shut. "Trust me. It's romantic."

"What were you going to say, Cole?" She was ravenous for information about Mary, about Cole's relationship with her. Up until now, and that bit about Mary's freaking smile lighting up a room, the man had stayed annoyingly silent on the subject. "You met…?"

"Outside. In the winter." His Adam's apple bobbed with another deep swallow of his beer. "So…ah…there was snow. And where there's snow, there's kids doing snowlike stuff. The snow globe represents all of that. Therefore, it's romantic."

"Snowlike stuff is very romantic," she said as seriously as she could pull off. "I mean, come on. We have snow…and we have *stuff*. How did I miss that connection before?"

"Sarcasm, Rachel? Really?" he said in an annoyingly accurate imitation of her mother. She considered smacking his arm again but didn't. She flat-out didn't have the energy. Raising his hands in defeat, he said, "You tell me, then. What type of gift do you consider romantic?"

The answer came to her quickly. She reached under the table and grasped the bag she'd dropped by her feet. "This," she said softly, removing and then placing the vase on the table between them. "Combined with what you said, I consider this a romantic gift."

Something intense and dark entered his eyes, colored his expression. He leaned forward, propped his elbows on the table and seemed to look straight into her soul. Everything about the moment—the look and the man— seared into her, heating her from the inside out.

Longing struck, hard and fast, curling in her belly

and spreading through her entire body inch by inch, until every part of her trembled with need, with desire. Oh, no. This wouldn't do at all. Cole was taken. Heck, *she* was taken.

"You consider the vase a romantic gift?" Cole asked without dropping his gaze.

"Now who's repeating statements in the form of a question?" she asked in a light, breezy tone meant to mask her discomfort. "If you and I were involved in a relationship, then yes, I would consider the vase romantic and…sweet. Because of what you said about my eyes. But, you know, we're not involved in a relationship."

He held her eyes with his for another breath-stealing second before returning to his side of the table. "Same concept," he said, his voice just this side of gruff. "The sentiment is what's romantic, and therefore, the snowman is." Another wink and that good ole boy smirk. "I win."

"Yes," she said, giving up on her earlier denials. He'd proven his point. "You do." Then, seeing Cole's mom walking toward them with a tray laden with food, she relaxed. Surely, by the time they finished eating, her body would have returned to its normal, non-nuclear state. "Your mom is bringing our food," she said to Cole. "So behave."

"Why, darlin', I always behave," Cole said as he pivoted in his seat to greet his mother. "I didn't think you were working tonight or we would've come back and said hi."

"Two of our part-timers called in sick," Margaret said. She smiled at Rachel. "It's good to see you, sweetheart." Without asking which order belonged to who, she placed Cole's burger and thick-sliced chips in front of him and

Rachel's soup and salad in front of her. "Your parents in town for the holidays, or is it just you?"

"Mom will be here in a few days, I think." For some reason that Rachel didn't dare speculate on, she didn't mention Andrew. "Dad will probably be here soon after."

"That's nice. Families should be together during Christmas." Rumpling her son's hair with one hand, she said, "Did this one tell you we have family arriving next week? His aunt and uncle, their kids, their spouses and two babies. We'll have a full house."

"Uh, no. He didn't mention it, but that's great."

"I have an idea! You and your parents should join us for Christmas dinner," Margaret said. "We'll have plenty of food, and—as they say—the more the merrier. Think about it, won't you? We'd love to have you. Right, Cole?"

"Absolutely," Cole said. "Great idea, Mom."

"I...don't know what our plans are yet," Rachel said quickly. She would love nothing more than to be a part of the Fosters' Christmas, but *Mary* would certainly be there. With a diamond ring on her finger, no less. "But yes, I'll mention the invitation to my parents." Then, belatedly, she remembered to say, "Thank you for the invitation. It's very thoughtful."

Margaret balanced the now empty tray on one hip. "So, what are you two up to tonight?"

"Eating," Cole said shortly. "And then back to shopping."

"For his girlfriend," Rachel piped in, unable to stop herself. "I have discovered that your son is rather picky when it comes to selecting gifts."

Margaret laughed. "He's picky about a lot of things, not just shopping." She rumpled his hair again. "Women, for one. Why, I was beginning to wonder if he would ever fall in love. Or, for that matter, admit it once he had. Now that he has, I'm just so pleased."

"Mom," Cole said in a semi-warning sort of way. "I'm sure Rachel doesn't want to hear about any of this—"

"To the contrary!" Rachel inserted. Beaming a bright smile at Margaret, she gestured for her to continue. "Please, I'd love to hear more about Cole's girlfriend. He hasn't been that forthcoming as of yet."

"Oh, I adore her. She's intelligent and warm-hearted, has a great sense of humor, and frankly," Margaret said, tossing her son an indulgent look, "she might be the only woman in the world capable of going toe-to-toe with this one here. So yes, I'm delighted by his choice."

Well, there went the idea that his family didn't approve.

"That's great. Really, really great," Rachel said, attempting to keep the sourness on her tongue from leeching into her voice. "Really."

"Isn't it, though?" Nodding toward a customer at a nearby table who'd gestured for Margaret's attention, she said, "Well, work is calling. You two have a terrific rest of the evening. And Rachel? Please give your parents my best."

"I will," Rachel said as Cole's mom scurried off. "I've always liked your mother," she then said to Cole. "Your entire family, actually."

"They all like you, too."

The next several minutes were—thankfully—spent quietly eating. Strangely, as hungry as she'd been when they'd entered Foster's, now Rachel found she didn't have much of an appetite. Something was bugging her, but she couldn't quite put her finger on what.

Well, okay. She couldn't say she'd come to terms with Cole falling in love, because she hadn't. But that didn't fully explain the weird vibe she had. She picked at her salad, trying to decide what, exactly, had set her instincts on high alert.

It was right there, lurking on the edge of her consciousness, but despite how hard she tried, she couldn't quite grasp the knowledge and bring it home. She sighed and gave up. She was tired, frustrated, and her feet hurt. Maybe later, after a good night's sleep, her subconscious would connect the pieces and arrive at a conclusion.

Or perhaps, she was simply insanely jealous when she had no reason or right to be.

Stupid, that. So, so stupid.

"Tell me," she said as she pierced a slice of cucumber with her fork, "more about Mary."

"Sure. What do you want to know?"

"Anything other than obscure, meaningless details."

Cole gave her a pointed look. "If you ask a direct question, I'll give you a direct answer. As long as it doesn't relate to Mary's identity, I'm an open book."

Okay, now that she had his attention and his willingness to actually talk, what did she want to know? "How long have you two known each other?"

"Since we were children."

Oh. She hadn't expected that answer. "Do *I* know her?"

"I…feel fairly sure you'd recognize her."

"By name or by face?"

"Both."

Oh again. "What does she do for a living?"

"Nope." Cole took a bite of his hamburger. After he'd chewed and swallowed, he said, "Answering that question could put you on the scent to who she is, which I don't want you to know just yet. So ask something else."

Brat. He'd always been too smart for his own good. "What does she do in her free time?"

He shrugged. "Same stuff anybody does, I guess. Depends on the day and her mood."

"Dammit, Cole! That is not a concrete answer."

"Then ask me some concrete questions, Rach."

Glowering, she stabbed a chunk of chicken from her salad and chewed it rather vehemently. "Fine. Say it's raining outside and she doesn't have to work, what does she do?"

"What do you do when it's raining outside?" he countered.

"Read books, go to the movies, get chores done," she said without thinking. "Nap if I'm tired. Scour the internet. Talk to friends. Any one of a million possibilities."

"There's your answer. Don't look so surprised. By and large, people are similar."

"I give up," she muttered. "Why don't you tell me whatever you feel like sharing?"

"I can do that." He took a drink from his beer, leaned back in his chair and cradled his arms behind his head. "Did I tell you about her smile?"

"You did." *One. Two. Three.* She made it to ten without screaming, so said, "How about we start with the three traits you love the most about her, and then move on to three that you're not so fond of? Perhaps that will help me get a handle on her. That is, if you still want my help in romancing her. Otherwise, I'm done, Cole. I can't give advice without any information."

"Sorry. You're absolutely right." He ran a hand over his jaw. "I guess this is more difficult for me than I thought it would be. It isn't easy, sharing how you feel for—or view—another person, especially someone you care so much for."

Her simmering temper cooled. That, she understood. "Okay. I get that."

"Three traits, huh? Well, I love how she cares about other people. She's compassionate. Tends to puts herself into predicaments that make her nuts, even hurt her, but she does it anyway. Out of love, I guess. I find that remarkable, seeing how—for most folks—the self-protection instinct reigns above all else."

"That's a good one," Rachel admitted. And it was. She liked to think of herself as compassionate, but look at how she'd behaved with her mother earlier that day? So, whether she liked it or not, Mary beat her out in this regard. Ugh. "Compassion is important."

"Yup." Closing his eyes, Cole released a breath. "Let's see, what else?" His eyes popped open. "I'm assuming you're not interested in the physical traits that…I…er, appreciate?"

"I've already assumed she's attractive, so no. Not interested." Lie. Big fat lie, at that. Rachel would give half—no *all*—of the money in her bank account to know exactly *how* attractive Mary was. But to admit that… uh-uh. Besides which, she'd meet the woman someday and would be able to see for herself.

"Well, she's more than attractive, Rach. She's…drop-dead gorgeous. And that's a fact."

"Of course she is," Rachel all but purred. "I can't imagine you falling for a less-than-gorgeous woman. You've always been a little too hung-up on looks."

He squinted his eyes. "Not true."

"True." Rachel waved her fork in the air. "Every girlfriend you've ever had could've been a centerfold model. Heck, a few of them were, weren't they?"

"Yup, but a few of your past men were…runway models? Is that the term?"

"But they had more than one thought in their heads. Can't say the same for...what was her name? Bootsie? Bitsie? Barbie?"

"Brinley. Her name was Brinley, and I think you're being unfair. She had, oh—" Cole stopped for a second, grinned "—two thoughts, at least. On some days, she'd even make it to three. But I'm willing to agree that I appreciate a beautiful woman. How's that?"

"Appreciate? Why—" Rachel snapped her jaw shut. This wasn't getting her anywhere. "Good enough. Trait two, please?"

"Right. Back to business. She makes me laugh. Whenever we're together, no matter what we're doing, laughing is almost always involved. I like that in anyone, but especially in a woman I'm considering spending the rest of my life with."

"She's funny? That ranks in your top three important traits?"

"Naturally. Would you want to spend your life with someone who was boring?"

"Well...no. But I'm not sure I'd rank it in my top three." Honesty. Integrity. Trust. Those were her top three. Wanting children would come next, then...okay, then yeah, someone who could make her laugh. Someone who could see the light in the darkness and help lead her there, when she needed it. "Top five, though."

"See? We're not so different." An inquisitive gleam entered his eyes. She was sure he was going to ask about her top three, but he didn't. Instead, he said, "And behind curtain number three—Mary makes me want to be a better man. In every way possible."

"Why? What is it about her that does that to you?" This was crucial. This, Rachel knew, was the real, true reason Cole was in love with this woman. And God help her, but she needed to understand. Not only because of her conflicted emotions toward him, about *them,* but because maybe, just maybe, she'd finally be able to grasp what wasn't right in her relationship with Andrew. Or, for that matter, her parents' relationship. Because they certainly didn't seem to bring out the best in each other. "Because yes, that's…well, it's essential, isn't it? But why?"

The question seemed to perplex him, as evidenced by his knotted brow and quick intake of breath. "Now that, Rach, is a damn good question. I'm not sure if I can answer it, though. It's intrinsic. Knowing her, being close to her, brings out my better self. I don't know why." He flattened his hands against the table, on either side of his plate. "It just *is*."

She nodded, as if she understood, when in truth, she felt more confused than ever. Andrew was a terrific man in many, many ways. He cared about her, she knew. But did she make him feel the way Cole felt about Mary? Did Rachel bring out the best in Andrew?

Of course, the more compelling question—the one Rachel really needed to answer—was did Andrew bring out the best in her? Did he make *her* want to be a better person?

In some ways, sure. Mostly, though…mostly, it was Cole who did that to her. And no, like him, she couldn't say *why*. Like him, it was just that way—had *always* been that way.

"Does Andrew do for you what Mary does for me?" Cole asked, as if reading her thoughts. He'd always been irritating that way.

"Yes," she whispered. "Of course he does." Then, because she couldn't bear any further discussion on Mary or Cole's feeling for her at the moment, she glanced at her watch. "Ooh, look at the time! We'll have to put off the rest of this conversation for later. If we want to hit up any additional stores tonight, we better get moving."

"Sounds good," Cole said easily enough, pulling himself to his feet. "But I do have a few concerns about Mary I want to talk over with you. *Serious* concerns. Just to get your take, you understand. In case I'm not seeing things in the right light. Women confuse the hell out of me."

"Yes, you've mentioned that." She followed suit and stood, put on her coat and retrieved her precious vase. Serious concerns? Why the hell was he proposing if he had serious concerns? "Tomorrow, then. We'll get into the rest. I...I'm more than happy to help you see things in the right light. If I can."

Doubtful, but hey—that's what friends were for, right? Right.

"If you can't, then no one can." Cole wrapped his arm securely around her waist. "You, Rachel Merriday," he said with a kiss—a freaking *peck*—on the top of her head, "are a true gem. Andrew is one helluva lucky guy. Why, if I didn't have Mary, I'd be downright jealous."

She almost said that she had Andrew and she was still jealous, just to see how he'd react. She didn't, though. Couldn't. Because what woman in her right mind would set herself up for public humiliation and heartbreak? None that she knew.

One thing was becoming clear. If she couldn't get a handle on her emotions, she'd have to get the hell out of Steamboat Springs as soon as humanly possible. Otherwise, she might not be able to stop herself from falling completely, irrevocably in love with the wrong man.

How ironic was it that she'd arrived in Steamboat Springs with the goal of giving her heart to Andrew, only to discover that Cole still owned a decent-sized chunk of it? It was incredibly unfair. Depressing. Pitiful. And, Rachel thought, an absolutely no-win situation.

On all accounts.

Chapter Six

Saturday dawned bright and sunny with nary a snow-flake in the sky. With Andrew's work crisis momentarily solved and a perfect day for skiing awaiting them, Rachel called Cole and canceled their planned shopping trip. She didn't lie, either. Told him that since she'd spent all of yesterday with him, she owed Andrew some one-on-one time.

Surprisingly, he didn't argue. Of course, that could be because they'd actually made some headway last night in purchasing gifts for Mary. He'd bought a photo album that he planned on filling with pictures—or as he had called them, memories—of he and Mary, of their "journey so far," along with a camera to "capture more memories" with.

She couldn't negate the romance quotient of either of those choices, even if the whole idea caused her stomach to hurt.

Next, he'd chosen a bottle of *Rachel's* favorite perfume, saying that he didn't know offhand what Mary's scent was, and he liked Rachel's, so why not? Sure. Why not? Soon, Cupcake would be prancing around with the fragrance Rachel had worn for the past *five freaking years* squirted behind her ears. Lovely. Just lovely.

She'd thrown her personal bottle away the second she'd arrived home. Then, feeling guilty over being wasteful, she yanked it out of the trash. She had no intention of wearing that particular fragrance ever again, but maybe Haley would.

So, after the memory-making conversation and the perfume debacle, Rachel hadn't had the energy to object when Cole dragged her into the hardware store for the final gift of the day. Well, okay. She was also quite curious to see what type of hardware Cole would deem romantic. A flashlight, apparently. A huge, heavy, spotlight of a flashlight. Why? She didn't have a clue and she didn't bother asking. She'd learned her lesson on that one.

Today, though, she didn't have to think about that. Tomorrow, either. Her only plan for the entire weekend was to relax, enjoy herself and bolster her connection with Andrew. Monday—when she and Cole had now decided to finish their shopping extravaganza—would roll around soon enough. Hopefully, by then, she'd have put every last issue into perspective.

And if she hadn't? Well, she'd tell Andrew she'd changed her mind and wanted to go to Hawaii. He'd be pleased, her promise to Cole would be fulfilled and her parents could have an empty house to wage war in. Though she'd wait until her father arrived. Despite Rachel's unwillingness to become the tennis ball again, she couldn't leave her mother here alone.

She shook her head to clear her thoughts. If she didn't hurry, Andrew would be on the phone with the office again—just checking to be sure everything was still "good-to-go." Rachel ran the brush through her hair, applied a touch of makeup, gave herself a quick once-over in the mirror and considered the job done.

They'd start with breakfast out, hit the slopes for a few hours, grab a late lunch, and if Andrew's schedule still remained free—which she very much hoped would be the case—they'd finally see about getting a tree. All in all, the day's prospects looked bright.

"I'm ready," she called out as she headed down the stairs. She expected to find Andrew in the kitchen or maybe in the living room. He was in neither. With a heavy sense of foreboding, she cracked open the office door.

Andrew sat behind her father's desk with his phone pressed to his ear, concentrating on whatever appeared on his laptop. He looked up, saw Rachel and smiled. Holding up one finger, he whispered, "Sorry, darling. This shouldn't take long."

And that, Rachel knew, could mean anything from five minutes to two hours to all day. She nodded and pivoted on her heel. She'd make some coffee, check her email to see if her mother had made flight arrangements yet and…wait.

"You're *letting* her spend the day with that man?" Haley asked Cole with her hands planted on her narrow hips. "Are you crazy? You might as well wrap her up in a bright red bow and gift her to him. Geez, Cole. I thought you were in love with Rachel."

"She has to be able to freely choose." Cole turned and escaped the confines of the small office at the back of the store. Seeing how his plans with Rachel were canceled, he figured he'd give Haley the day off and work the shift she'd already agreed to work for him. "Don't you have friends to spend the day with?" he said over his shoulder. "You're free, kid. Shoo."

His sister trailed after him. The store didn't open for another thirty minutes, which meant she would badger him until the second he unlocked the door. He wasn't exactly happy that Rachel had canceled, but what he'd said to his sister was true. There were many, many actions he was more than willing to take to achieve his goal, but he refused to do anything that could potentially hinder Rachel's ability to choose.

That was paramount. If he were fortunate enough to have this whole mess work out well, then he needed to know she'd chosen him for the right reasons. And yup, that meant stepping back and understanding that she currently had a boyfriend she wanted to spend time with.

Even if the images of what they might be doing together just about killed him.

"You're pitifully lacking in the how-a-female-thinks department, aren't you?" Haley asked, skidding to a stop next to him. "If there was a man that I 'might' have feelings for, and I canceled a date with him, and he didn't utter one word of complaint, I'd think he couldn't care less. So, I'd do everything I could to expunge my feelings for him."

"Hmm," Cole murmured in a non-committal way. Food for thought, he supposed. But not enough to alter his decision. "It wasn't a date. Technically speaking."

"*And* if I had canceled said date to spend time with another man, that man would suddenly appear much more interesting to me than he had before. Interesting enough that I might forget all about man number one and focus all of my loving attention on man number two."

"Too much information." Haley might be a full-grown adult, but she was still his baby sister. He had no desire to hear about her bestowing her loving attention on any man. No matter how generic the description might be. "What would you have me do? Kidnap her?"

"Um, no. That would just tick her off." She tapped her bottom lip with one finger. "Unless…you know, if you did it right, a kidnapping *could* be romantic."

"While I adore you and thank you kindly for your advice, I believe I'll avoid breaking the law," Cole said with a laugh. "You really don't have anything better to do today? Because if not, I'm sure I can find other ways to occupy myself. Or I can always call Mom. She mentioned last night that several employees were out sick."

Like all the Fosters, Haley helped where help was needed, but her main role in the family businesses was more detail oriented. She took care of the books, purchased supplies, updated the websites and kept everyone else organized.

"Unfair." She wrinkled her nose. "I was there all last weekend, on top of a full week in the office. I know Reid is off somewhere saving the day, but where's Dylan?"

Cole chuckled again at the reference to their oldest brother. Reid did his duty by the family, but his primary gig—especially during the winter months—was as a member of the national ski patrol. So yep, Reid was very likely saving the day somewhere.

"I don't know where Dylan is. Shall I phone Mom and ask?"

"No, no," Haley said quickly. "I have plenty to do, thank you very much."

He gestured toward the front door. "Then what are you still doing here?"

"Leaving!" With a quick grin and a wave, she hot-footed it across the store, only to stop three short steps from freedom. "Did Mom mention how many employees are out sick?"

"Go. Have. Fun," Cole ordered his sister. "If Mom really needs you, she'll let you know. You've put in more hours than anyone else the past two weeks, and we all know it."

Facing him, she shrugged. "My social life is fairly bleak at the moment. Working is better than sitting at home being bored out of my skull. And I like helping."

"I know you do. So, how about a compromise? Do something fun for a few hours and then check in with the folks?" He grinned, thinking of the dinner-table conversation the other night. "Go lurk in the bookstore and see what you can do about livening up your social life."

"Ah...no." A rash of red spread over Haley's cheeks. He knew his sister well enough to recognize the flush of anger, not embarrassment, when he saw it. "That's over."

"That was quick. Didn't you just go out last night?" he asked in a genial tone. "Did something happen, or just a change of heart?"

"Something happened, but it isn't important enough to discuss."

He gave her a closer look, didn't like what he saw, and concern rode in to replace his earlier amusement. "Haley?"

"Cole?" she fired back.

"You know I'll get it out of you eventually, so you might as well spill." He waited, she didn't speak, so he said, "You two did have a date last night, correct?"

"Yes," she said in a low, I-don't-want-to-talk-about-this voice.

"And?"

"I'm fine, Cole." He didn't speak, just worried. Watched her wrap her hair around her finger. Ten seconds later, with a stubborn lift of her chin, she said, "He was a little too touchy-feely for a first date and he didn't seem to comprehend the word 'no,' which ticked me off."

It ticked Cole off, too. But unlike his two older brothers, he had zero doubts that their sister could take care of herself. "I assume you…taught him the meaning of the word 'no'?"

"Oh, yes," she said with a wide grin. "In no uncertain terms."

"Good." He might have to pay a visit to the bookstore later. Just to be sure. "Let me know if he requires another lesson."

"Will." She started to turn toward the door again, but stopped. In a too-casual-to-be-casual way, she said, "This guy came by yesterday to see you. He might try again today. He was curious if you were hiring any ski instructors for the season. I told him I didn't know what your plans were, but that he should talk to you."

"I think we're all set this year, but if he stops in, I'll get his name for next."

"His name is Gavin. Gavin Daugherty," Haley filled in. "From what he said, I believe he recently moved here. He…ah… Are you sure we couldn't use one more instructor?"

"I'm sure."

"Really, really sure?"

Cole narrowed his eyes. "Yes, Haley. Why?"

"I don't know. I… He's new here."

"You mentioned that."

"So he probably needs a job, and…" She trailed off, darted her gaze to the side of Cole's. Her cheeks, which had resumed their normal color, grew pink again. This time, though, her blush had zip to do with anger. "You know what?" she said in a huff. "Forget I even mentioned it."

"Gavin…Daugherty? That his name? I'll be sure to tell him you said hi. If he were to drop in today, that is." Cole walked behind the sales counter and grabbed a pad of paper, scrawled Mr. Daugherty's name in oversize letters. "There. Now I'll be sure to remember."

Certain things, like teasing your younger sister, never grew old.

"You do that," Haley said with a sweet-as-sugar smile. "Okay, I'm off. I wonder if Rachel is around? Might just call her and see if today's a good day for that visit."

"Go for it," he said with an equally sweet smile. "She'll probably be happy to see you."

"We might have a nice, long chat," Haley said. "I'm sure the topic of men will come up. It almost always does, you know. And relationships. Us women *love* to talk about men…who they're dating, who they used to date, why are they dating that person, and so on."

"Cool. Have fun," Cole said without concern. Haley would never rat him out.

She wrinkled her nose again. "You're not worried in the slightest, are you?"

"Nope."

"Figures." She paused, nervously ran her fingers through her shoulder-length hair. Then, "You won't mention me to Gavin either, right?"

"Nope," Cole repeated. "But you knew that."

"I did," she affirmed, but he didn't quite believe her. "Be nice to him, okay, Cole? Let him down easy. He seemed...I don't know, sort of lost and...just promise you'll be nice."

Ah. Well, that explained it. Haley was a sucker for picking up strays. That, believe it or not, caused Cole greater concern than what he'd learned about her prior evening's date. Between Reid, Dylan and Cole, Haley had been taught how to take care of herself in sticky situations.

But none of them had yet to figure out how to protect her from herself, from her soft heart or her frustrating penchant for diving in to problems—i.e., involving herself with people she thought she could "save"—that should be avoided.

Even so, he knew better than to say another word on the topic.

"I'm not typically mean to anyone," he pointed out, hoping that would suffice. There was a world of difference between "mean" and "nice," and until he met this "lost" man who'd caught his sister's eye, he would be very careful with any promises regarding him.

She frowned. Stared at him for all of three seconds before coming to a conclusion. Giving up the pretense of leaving, she stalked toward the office. "Dang it all! I guess you're stuck with me for a few hours. I...ah...forgot to place those orders last week. Better do so now."

"Slacking during our busy season, really?" he asked, playing along with the appropriate amount of sarcasm. "Wow, sis. That doesn't sound like you. You're normally so...efficient and organized. Something must have been on your mind? Or...someone?"

"Bite me," she growled seconds before disappearing into the office.

"And typically more eloquent," he called out loudly. Her response was a resounding slam of the office door. Cole glanced at the pad of paper with Gavin Daugherty's name written on it. If the man didn't come around today, Cole would grab a coffee at the Beanery and quiz Lola. She knew everyone.

And then, he'd see if he had cause to be concerned or not.

Rachel stared longingly at the skiers traveling up the mountain on chairlifts and even more longingly at those she could spy zipping back down. Andrew had been true to his word—his phone call had been quick, and breakfast had been pleasant. They'd relaxed, chatted about this and that, and a full hour-and-a-half had gone by without his phone ringing once.

Unfortunately, Cole had nailed it when he'd offered to take Andrew to the bunny slope. As fit and athletic as Andrew was, he simply was not a natural skier. It didn't make any sense. He loved sports, went on a white-water rafting trip every summer with some of his friends, spent almost as much time in the gym as he did at work and enjoyed running.

Skiing, however, was not progressing well.

"Okay," she said after they'd sidestepped to the top of the gentle slope for the—oh, tenth or so time. "Try to remember to keep your head up, so you can see where you're going. Keep your skis parallel with each other, and don't be afraid to use your poles for balance."

"I understand the basics, Rachel," Andrew said, frustration evident in his demeanor and his voice. "I just don't seem to be able to put that understanding to practical use."

"What, exactly, are you having problems with?"

"I would have to say…skiing."

She almost laughed. With Cole, she would've. But

Andrew rarely joked. "Perhaps we should stick with flat ground for a while," Rachel said, trying to remember the long, long ago day she'd first learned to ski. Her father had taught her. It happened to be one of her better memories. "You can practice sliding backward and forward, get a better feel of how the skis respond without going downhill. We probably should've started with that."

She would've, for sure, if she hadn't been under the impression that Andrew had already learned the basics. As it was, the thought hadn't occurred to her.

"I'm sorry. This can't be very enjoyable for you," Andrew said, jabbing his poles hard into the snow. "But I'll figure it out."

"Spending any time with you is enjoyable," Rachel said firmly. And of course, that was true. What type of person would she be if it weren't? "And you'll absolutely get the hang of skiing. At some point, you'll quit thinking so hard and your body will just react instinctively." She smiled and slid forward, patted Andrew's arm. "Until then, we'll keep practicing."

"Keep falling, you mean," Andrew said, surprising her with an actual joke. "But okay. Flat ground, huh?"

"For a while. Until you feel a little more comfortable. First, though," she said, jerking her chin toward the small slope they stood on top of, "we have to get to the bottom again."

"I have a feeling I'm using muscles I didn't know existed, and that I'll feel every one of those muscles tomorrow." He nodded, breathed in deeply and carefully slid into place. "Here I go. Head up, skis parallel, use poles for balance."

"Yep. Just push off gently, once or twice, and let the snow carry you. Remember to lean forward and vee the skis as you approach the bottom, in order to stop."

Andrew quirked an eyebrow. "Or," he said drily, "I can use the veer-out-of-control-until-you-lose-your-balance-and-crash-to-a-stop method. I've found that works quite well."

"Was that two jokes in a row, Mr. Serious?" She grinned and let her amusement bubble into a laugh. "Wedge your skis, balance your weight forward a tad, and you won't fall. Promise."

"Uh-huh, if you say so." He pulled in another breath, nodded and pushed off. She waited before following, mentally crossing her fingers and darn-near holding her breath to see if he'd make it to the bottom without his typical crash landing.

He went down the slope easily enough, but as he approached the bottom, his body swayed forward a smidgen too far, and he veered wildly to the left. She was sure he was going to fall, again, but he managed to catch his balance and come to an awkward, skidding halt.

Still standing, even. He turned toward her and raised his poles in a celebratory gesture. Her smile widened and she returned the gesture before sliding down to meet him.

"See? This isn't so hard," she said when she stopped next to him. "Before too long, you'll find this little ole slope boring as all get out and you'll wonder why you ever thought skiing was difficult. Heck, I bet we'll be up there—" she pointed toward the peak she'd been eyeing earlier "—before Christmas."

Andrew's ruddy-from-the-cold complexion blanched. "That sounds terrific, Rachel. I only hope you won't be overly disappointed if that doesn't happen. I... Well, I don't seem to have a natural inclination toward skiing, now do I?"

She pieced together their various conversations,

thought of the recreational activities he *didn't* take part of—such as mountain climbing and bungee jumping—and suddenly, she got it. "You're afraid of heights, aren't you?"

"I'm not afraid," he said with a slight lift of his shoulders. "I just don't particularly like them, which is why I've never bothered to learn how to ski. It isn't a huge deal."

"Cole's wrong. Women aren't confusing, men are." She shook her head, exasperated. "Why did you let me drag you here, then, Andrew? There is plenty for us to do on vacation. Skiing does not have to be one of our activities."

"You enjoy the sport. I...was trying to make you happy." He shrugged again in a stiff, almost embarrassed manner. "I enjoy your happiness."

"I can be just as happy doing something else," she said as warmth and contentment settled over her. Andrew truly was a great guy. A solid, dependable man who had a lot to give the right woman. She *wanted* to be that woman. It would make perfect sense.

She waited for her pulse to speed up, for her heart to melt and her knees to shake...for anything other than the sweet simplicity of warmth and contentment to envelop her. None of which occurred. Why not? Why couldn't she feel more for Andrew?

What she did feel...was that enough? She didn't know, but she was beginning to believe that might be the best she could attain. Not only with Andrew, though.

With any man who wasn't Cole.

"Let's get out of here," she said, refusing to dwell on what she could never have. "We're going to find a Christmas tree."

"Thank God," Andrew said with a relieved grin. He

bent down to unclasp the bindings on his skis, and then one by one, stepped out of them. When he stood straight again, he pulled her to him for a kiss. A long, slow kiss that should have set her blood on fire.

But…no. Not even a flicker. The absence of that surprised her. Oh, their kisses had never ignited a blazing inferno, but they'd certainly held heat. Now, though, she felt nothing. Not even a barely there spark. What had happened?

Instinctively, and without considering how Andrew might take it, she yanked herself out of his hold and removed her skis. "I was thinking after the tree, we could—"

"What's wrong, Rachel?" Andrew asked.

"Nothing's wrong!" she lied. "We're in public, for one thing. And… Well, I'm excited about getting a tree and decorating. I've wanted to for days, you know."

She hadn't meant to infer anything about Andrew's workaholic nature, or even how he'd barely left her father's office for the past two days. Truly. Her goal had only been to offer an excuse for her behavior, to give her some space that would then allow her to consider where, if anywhere, she wanted their relationship to go. To decide…the rest of her life, she supposed.

Andrew, however, read all the wrong things in her words. "I'm sorry I haven't been available," he said in a tight, controlled voice. "Perhaps with all the time you spent with Cole yesterday and the day before, the two of you should have chosen a tree."

"That wasn't what I meant. And he offered, but I told him no." She grabbed her skis and started to storm off, not sure if she was angry with Andrew or herself. "I told him I'd promised you, and that you and I would do so together."

He caught up to her quickly, gripped her shoulder gently. "Rachel, wait. I *am* sorry. I'd really like to have a nice day with you. In fact, I'll turn off my cell until... Monday. No interruptions for the rest of the weekend, how does that sound?"

"You don't have to do that," she said without turning around. "I really do understand how important your company is to you, Andrew. I don't want to stand in the way of that."

She expected him to reiterate his offer, to state unequivocally that he wanted nothing more than to spend a workless weekend with her. She should have known better.

"Thank you," he said without so much as a hint of a pause. "But I promise you'll have my undivided attention for the rest of the afternoon. Seems a fair compromise, doesn't it?"

"How about long enough to get a tree and help me bring up the boxes of decorations from downstairs?" She couldn't even be annoyed he'd backslid. Heck, if *she* wanted a workless weekend with Andrew, then she shouldn't have let him off the hook. "Maybe even hang an ornament or two. Does that sound agreeable?"

"Absolutely," Andrew said, coming around to stand beside her. He tipped her chin toward him and kissed her lightly on the lips. "Maybe even three or four. Though, I might need to pause in between two and three, for a quick phone call. Say two ornaments per call?"

"Hmm. I'd prefer three."

"Deal."

"Careful," Rachel said, "or I'll talk you into stringing the lights, as well."

The tension eased, thank goodness. They both laughed and headed in the general direction of the car.

Would a life with Andrew be one set of negotiations after another? She could almost hear them now, balancing how many nights he would work late as opposed to how many school plays or recitals he would attend.

A weekend business trip? Sure, honey, as long as you show up for the neighborhood barbecue we've planned. What? You'll be gone for a week? Well, then, how about that vacation we've been talking about for the past two years?

She was probably being unfair. Andrew tried to make time for her, had since they'd started dating. He'd be the same as a husband, a father. He'd...try. She didn't have any doubts about that. Except...well, *trying* wasn't quite the same as *doing,* now was it?

Cole wouldn't have to try, he'd just...do. She knew this because she knew him. Had seen how he behaved with his parents and his siblings for a large chunk of her life.

They were almost to the car when a realization slammed into being. Rachel jerked her body to a stop. Why had she thought the two men were so much alike? Good-looking, check. Good hearts, check. Both stood for what they believed in, check.

Now, though, she understood something she hadn't before, she saw the one trait that made Cole and Andrew as different as night and day. Andrew would always do his best by the people he loved and cared for, would always step up when he needed to. Of that, she also had no doubts. But Cole...Cole would never have to "step up."

He wouldn't need to. He'd already be there, next to the people—the woman—he loved, day in and day out, through everything that came their way.

And this she knew because that was how he was with *her,* his friend.

She thought back, to the days after Cole's accident, to everything that had happened. To the mind-numbing fear, the endless questions, the way he'd looked at her from his hospital bed. *His* fear when he learned his fall had likely ended his career.

He'd been lost. And she had been so scared, for him, for his future, but mostly by the desperation she'd glimpsed in his gaze. Their friendship had existed for years—their kiss was less than twenty-four hours old. At that moment, Rachel hadn't known how to be just his friend, and yet, she wasn't his girlfriend. She was caught somewhere in the middle, out of place, in uncharted territory that seemed larger and scarier as the hours ticked by.

Still, if it had not been for her father's phone call, she would've stayed. Somehow, someway, she would've forced herself to stay by Cole's side through every bit of everything he had to go through, despite her fear and her confusion of her place in his now vastly different world. Or maybe, over the course of time, she'd only convinced herself of that. She'd never know for sure, could only hope she'd have done what was right.

What she had done, though, was listen to her father when he told her that her mother had "gone off the deep end" and required Rachel's presence.

A mistake, leaving. But she had, indeed, left. Worse, she'd almost felt relieved, because with her parents she understood her role. She *knew* how to behave. She knew what they expected from her. That was the easy and familiar choice, so she took it.

And had regretted the decision ever since.

Her plan had been to return as soon as she'd dealt with her mother, but Cole had told her not to. Between her guilt at leaving in the first place and those words—

words that had hurt *her*—she'd listened and stayed away. Until last year, when he'd finally asked her to visit for Christmas. She never should have left, but she sure as hell should've come back.

If their roles had been reversed, Cole wouldn't have abandoned her for anything short of an all-out family emergency. He also would've returned the very second doing so became possible, despite anything she might have said.

He was like that. Steadfast and sure.

For the first time since learning of Cole's relationship with Mary, Rachel felt, if not happy, grateful that he'd found someone. She only hoped that Mary was the woman Cole deserved, the woman that Rachel should have been when he'd needed her the most.

It no longer mattered that Rachel had changed, that she wouldn't make the same mistakes today. Now, all she could do was focus on the future. She looked up, saw that Andrew had reached the car and had turned around, searching for her.

She waved and started walking toward him, toward a possible future that would include warmth and contentment, dinner-table negotiations and…well, very little skiing. It wasn't hard to imagine creating a nice, uncomplicated life with Andrew. They'd do well together.

But would it be enough? She'd like to think so. She really, really would. Somehow, though, she doubted that would be the case. She wanted more. And more meant…*more*. It meant knowing, to the very depths of your being, that you were with exactly the right person, and that you were exactly the right person for him.

Andrew was a great guy, yes. But no, she couldn't say—now understood she would *never* say—that he was exactly the right man for her. Only one man held that role. And…well, the fact that he'd found happiness with someone else didn't alter the truth of Rachel's life. Of what she wanted, dreamed for. Of what she refused to give up on.

She couldn't have Cole. Fine. She'd find a way to accept that depressing reality and move on, even if that possibility seemed ludicrous and impossible. But if she settled, if she surrendered her dreams in lieu of a sufficient life, *she* would never be happy.

Andrew deserved more, as well.

Oh, God. Was she really going to do this? Had she, in mere minutes, made a firm, final decision regarding her relationship with Andrew? She stopped again, breathed and started forward. Yes. As insane as it was, she had.

She reached the car where Andrew waited, considered putting off the conversation until after they'd spent their day together, but that seemed…wrong. For both of them.

Fine lines appeared in his brow as he appraised her. "I take it we're going to the house," he said with a small sigh. "Instead of tree shopping and Christmas decorating?"

Common sense, the basic need for survival, almost had her refuting his instincts, but images of a future she didn't want flipped through her mind, strengthening *her* instincts, and therefore, her decision. "That would be best. I'm sorry, Andrew. We should talk."

"Right. Well, I suppose I've been expecting this." He gave her a searching type of look. "We could have a nice life together, Rachel. I was hoping—"

"I know, Andrew," she said, her heart heavy. "I was hoping, too."

"Is it the job?"

"No. Not really."

"Is it Cole?"

She hesitated. "In a way, but not how you think."

"I don't understand, then. I thought—" Stopping, he shook his head. "Doesn't matter. Let's go. We'll finish this discussion at the house."

Neither of them spoke another word throughout the drive home. Once there, there wasn't a whole lot more to say. Andrew accepted her explanation, made flight arrangements for the following morning and then spent the rest of the day and the evening in her father's office.

It was, all in all, rather anticlimactic.

Chapter Seven

During the drive to the airport on Sunday morning, Andrew seemed to be in good spirits, checking his email and reading off bits of the daily news to her. Somewhat surprising, considering the circumstances. Three days ago, they'd been a couple. In the small, small gap of time in between then and now, they were going their separate ways.

Mind-boggling, really. And depressing as hell.

Rachel had woken in the throes of second-guessing her decision. Obviously, she'd lost her mind. What was so wrong with a sufficient life, anyway? She *could* find some type of happiness in that, couldn't she? Then, in the next second, she'd think of Cole, of how freaking happy he was with Mary, of how *his* smile lit up whenever he talked about her.

Jealousy came next. She'd give just about anything to be in Cupcake's shoes, even if it meant being called a name more suited for a toy poodle than a human being. That would bring her thoughts back around to Andrew, to her decision, and how the thought of being alone *and* without Cole seemed so much worse, lonelier and emptier, than going forward with Andrew.

For a good hour or so, as she showered and readied herself for the day, her mind circled through these and similar thoughts. Analyzing, comparing, considering. Almost getting to the point of asking Andrew to stay through Christmas, and then backing off again.

What had finally settled the matter once and for all was realizing a not-so-pleasant truth about herself: she almost always chose the easier route. If one path made her uncomfortable, she went the other way. If that route became bumpy, she took the next fork in the road she could find. And dammit, this time she wasn't going to do that.

This time, she chose the more difficult path because it was the *right* path.

She swallowed, switched on her left-hand turn signal and tried to think of something appropriate to say. Her mother had taught her many things, but what to discuss with the man you'd just broken up with as you drove him out of town was, sadly, not one of them.

"You don't have to be nervous, Rachel," Andrew said, reading her thoughts quite well as he powered off his phone. "I'm the same person I was when we got here."

"But we're not the same, and that's my fault," she told him. She wasn't the same either, though she hadn't yet figured out what that meant in practical terms. Only time would tell. "Are you really okay? I mean, you seem okay, but…"

"I'm fine. Disappointed, yes, but…as I said yesterday, I was expecting this."

"Expecting what, exactly?"

"The end of our relationship. You're in love with Cole." He said the words plainly, without a hint of discord or contention. "I had my suspicions in New York, but I wasn't completely sure until I saw the two of you together."

"I didn't even know…" She trailed off, realizing she'd just admitted verbally what she hadn't wholly admitted to herself yet. "Cole and I aren't… We're not… I mean, he's in love with someone else. I didn't end our relationship to be with him."

"So I gathered from our conversation last night." Andrew sighed. "I'm not going home a broken man. I care for you, Rachel, but I don't—"

"Love me?" she filled in.

"Love is a subjective term. I'm very fond of you."

Fond. He was *fond* of her? "You were talking about making a life together. You were jealous of Cole."

"Of course I was jealous. As I said, I had hopes for us. When it became apparent you had deeper feelings for another man, I reacted. I'm not proud of my behavior, Rachel."

"But why would you care if—" She swallowed again. This, too, was important for her to understand. "Why would you consider spending your life with someone you don't love?"

"You're a beautiful woman. Intelligent and kind." A sidelong glance showed a small grin flit across Andrew's face. "Usually patient. You comprehend the complexities and the importance of my career. You're involved in a myriad of charities and social functions. All of these attributes appeal to me, for what I'm looking for in a partner."

"I see." Why did this bother her? She'd broken up

with him, after all. "Basically, what you're telling me, is that being in love is at the bottom of your list?"

"It isn't even on my list."

"Why not?"

"I… Is this important?" he asked, his tone becoming abrupt.

At the airport now, Rachel located the correct airline and pulled into the passenger drop-off lane. "It isn't my business," she said, turning to face him. "But I'd like to understand."

His jaw clenched tight, and she didn't think he was going to give her an answer. But then, he nodded. "I was in love once, a long time ago. I put my life on hold for her, made choices that alienated my family. When the relationship came to the disastrous conclusion everyone but me knew it would, I decided to focus my attention on the more practical attributes of a successful relationship."

Well, that cleared up several lingering questions.

"I'm sorry," she said, responding to the pain in his eyes, rather than the steel in his voice. "I'm sorry you were hurt and I'm sorry I can't be what you want."

"I've made my peace with the past. You're wrong on the other, though. You *could* be exactly what I want," he said in a milder tone, "but I understand that isn't what you want. I really am accepting of that. There isn't any need to feel guilty."

"All right. I'll…try not to."

He leaned across the car to kiss her on the cheek, stroked his hand down the length of her hair. "I wish you'd reconsider."

She didn't respond right away, just waited to see if her earlier doubts would resurface. They didn't. "I wish," she said lightly, "that you'd give love another chance.

We never know what's waiting around the next corner. Maybe you'll find a woman you can love who also has every one of the practical attributes you mentioned earlier."

"Hmm," he said, returning to his side of the car. "I find that prospect highly unlikely, but I'll consider the idea."

"Good."

They retrieved Andrew's luggage, said their goodbyes and promised to stay in touch. Whether they would or not was anyone's guess, but with Andrew, Rachel thought that might be nice. Someday, though. In the vast and foggy future that awaited them.

But that day wasn't today. Rachel put the car into Drive and left the airport while considering her options for the endless hours that stretched ahead of her. She'd get a tree, she decided. Maybe do a little shopping for some necessary items: scotch tape, wrapping paper, gift tags, lights for the tree and a few other odds and ends.

Not the least of which was a new brand of perfume.

Settling into a crouch, Cole went to work at straightening the pile of winter boots left in disarray after the morning rush. At the moment, Dylan was helping customers and manning the register, while Haley had her head bent over the computer in the office. Presumably up to her ears doing something "very important."

Or, more likely, still waiting for one Gavin Daugherty to appear.

Cole had stopped in at the Beanery on Sunday to talk with Lola. Since his questions had amused her more than anything else, he'd set his concerns on the back burner for now. His sister was an adult, for one thing. For another, he had plenty on his agenda to deal with.

Anticipation, along with a fair dose of anxiety, pooled in his gut as the clock ticked closer and closer to eleven. Unless she canceled again, he and Rachel were supposed to finish shopping today. He didn't want to shop. He wanted to spend a few hours outside, breathing in the fresh air. Maybe burn off some of his pent-up energy.

Changing their plans shouldn't be difficult. Rachel would rather do just about anything than mosey around a store for hours on end. Unless, of course, she waltzed in here fixated on finishing what they'd started, so she could run home to Andrew…to bestow more of her loving attention on him. Or, he supposed, to receive some of that loving attention herself.

"Pitiful," he muttered, rising. And adolescent, to boot. What Rachel did in her own time was her business, even if it damn well felt like it should be Cole's business, too.

He made his way to the front of the store, where Dylan was in the process of ringing up a customer. Their earlier crowd had thinned to a meandering few, none of whom appeared to be looking for anything specific. Wanderers, he liked to call them.

Wanderers were good, though. They often spent more money than folks who were looking for something specific. They also tended to be easier going, which was always a plus.

Dylan handed the customer his purchase, wished him a Merry Christmas, and once the man had left the store, whistled under his breath. "What's up with Haley? She about bit my head off this morning, all because I mentioned that I was surprised to see her here."

"No clue," Cole said, glancing out the window. No sign of Rachel yet.

"Well, did you ask her to come in today or something?"

"Nope. She was here when I got here."

Dylan narrowed his green eyes. "What aren't you saying?"

Geez. His brother always seemed to know when someone was hiding something, whether that something was big or small. This, Cole concluded, was a small matter that didn't require Reid's or Dylan's input. At least, not yet. Going for an innocent look, Cole shrugged. "I really have no idea what's bugging her. Maybe you irritated her?"

"Hmm. Suspiciously vague *and* trying to place blame elsewhere," Dylan said. "Both tactics make me very curious."

Ignoring the insinuation, Cole reached for and then flipped over the pad of paper with Gavin's name written on it. "This guy might come in this afternoon, asking about a job. If so, get his number and I'll get back to him in a few days."

Dylan glanced at the pad, nodded. "Sure. And hey, good attempt at changing the subject. Unfortunately, little brother, you have a tell when you're not being upfront."

"I am being upfront, and I don't know what you think you saw, but—" Cold air blew into the store when the door opened. Rachel, carrying two cups of coffee, swept in, her eyes bright and her cheeks pink. Relief unfurled inside. She hadn't canceled. Whew.

"Hey there, Rachel," Dylan said. "You brought me a coffee? How sweet."

"Hey, back. Actually," she said, handing one of the cups to Cole, "this is from Lola. When she learned I was on my way here, she insisted."

Knowing Lola as well as he did, Cole lifted the lid

and took a cautious, experimental sniff. "It smells sweet. What is it?"

"Eggnog latte." She grinned. "As I said, Lola insisted."

"Yuck." Cole passed the coffee to Dylan. "How's Lola today?"

"Good. Something odd happened, though." Rachel spoke the words lightly enough, but a nuance in her voice set off a cacophony of warning bells.

"Is that so? What type of odd?"

"Oh, it's probably nothing. I mentioned our plans for the day, how we were shopping for your girlfriend, and Lola was…well, I guess stunned would be the right way to put it." Rachel flicked an imaginary speck of lint off her coat. "She said that as far as she knew, you hadn't dated anyone since a year ago last fall."

"Huh. That is odd." Cole bent over, pretending to tie his shoe. Why hadn't he thought of this possibility? Lola *would* know if he was involved with someone, and Rachel loved coffee. She loved the Beanery. Hell, she adored Lola. "You're sure that's what Lola said?" he asked, standing straight. "Maybe she was talking about Dylan here, or…maybe Reid?"

Rachel sipped her coffee, eyeing him with confusion. "We were talking about you. She even went so far as to say that you're in the Beanery almost every day. Usually alone."

Dylan coughed loudly, trying to smother a laughing fit. He failed.

Crap. Was she on to him? Already? "Easy enough to explain," Cole said, avidly avoiding Dylan's gaze. "I… that is, Cupcake and I, have kept our relationship quiet. For the most part. Except for, er, family. Besides, I already told you how shy she is."

More muffled laughter from his brother. He was so going to kill him.

"Right. And determined." Rachel glanced from Cole to Dylan and back to Cole. "I thought of that possibility, since you're such a private type of guy, but one thing perplexes me."

He gave her a winning smile and gestured for her to go on.

"Lola and your mom are pretty close friends, right? Your mom seemed excited you were in a relationship, and when moms are excited about their kids, they...well, they tell their friends. So, for the life of me, I can't figure out why she wouldn't share this exciting news with Lola."

"Oh, she wanted to. Trust me on that," Cole said quickly. "I asked everyone in the family to keep quiet on the subject." Now, he looked at his brother. "You remember that conversation, don't you, Dylan?"

"Yup," he said. "By the way, it's nice to see you, Rachel. How's life treating you?"

Cole relaxed slightly. Maybe he wouldn't kill Dylan, after all.

Blink, blink. Pause. Blink. "Life's fine. Nice to see you, too. Anyway—"

"When you walked in, Cole and I were talking about tells, and how—" he winked at Cole "—Reid and Haley have fairly obvious ones, but Cole's took me a lot longer to figure out."

Just that fast, Cole was back to wanting to strangle his brother.

"Tells?" Rachel asked. "As in...?"

"You know, mannerisms that people fall into when they're...fibbing or skirting around a topic they'd prefer not to discuss," Dylan said with a jerky nod toward the back office. "Now, Haley, she twists her hair around her finger and avoids looking directly at you. Reid, on the other hand, shoots his gaze up and to the right. Every single time."

"That's crazy that you know that stuff," Cole said, just in case his brother had noticed something. "For the record, though, I don't have a tell."

"Does he?" Rachel asked Dylan.

"He does," Dylan confirmed. "But you have to watch closely, or you'll miss—"

"Rachel!" Haley half screeched as she exited the office. Good timing on her part. Glaring at her brothers as she approached, she said, "Nice job, guys, letting me know she was here."

The two women greeted each other, taking turns giving and accepting compliments, and chatting about this and that. While they did their thing, Cole glowered at Dylan, hoping he got the message. He didn't think he had a tell, but if he did, he'd prefer his brother—considering the current circumstances—keep those details secret.

Dylan leaned against the back counter and stretched his legs out in front of him. Giving a paused, pointed look at Rachel, he blinked rapidly as if something were stuck in his eye and then returned his gaze to Cole. "Tell," he mouthed.

Cole shook his head and glowered harder, if that were possible. People blinked constantly, for a variety of reasons that had nothing to do with subterfuge. Now, thanks to his know-it-all brother, Cole would wonder about every one of Rachel's blinks.

Just what he needed on top of everything else.

The women talked for a few more minutes—planning a day and a time for Haley to drop by for those clothes she wanted so much—before Cole and Rachel were able to make their escape. Outside, Cole filled his lungs with air and exhaled loudly.

"I don't want to shop," he said. "Feel up to putting that off for tomorrow?"

"I thought you were in a hurry?"

"I'm set with gifts through Wednesday, remember? As long as I have the rest by then, I'm good. Also," he said, thinking quickly, "I'm not exactly sure what else I want to get. Maybe we can come up with some more ideas today, make the actual shopping less tedious."

Rachel tipped her head back and laughed. It was, Cole reflected, a beautiful sound. "Uh-huh. What happened to 'this is special shopping, and it's Christmas, and I'm so, so excited'?"

"I did not say 'so, so.'" Following his instincts, Cole grabbed Rachel's hand. "Play with me today. Let's do something fun. For old time's sake."

"Wh-what did you have in mind?" she stammered.

"I was thinking…sledding. If you're up for it, of course."

"Oh, I'm up for it." Clichéd, maybe, but he'd have sworn her eyes sparkled just a little brighter at the prospect. "I'm assuming you have a couple of sleds lying around somewhere?"

"Of course I do." Another thought occurred. "Or… we could go snow-tubing—"

"Tubing?" Now, her voice held the same sparkle her eyes did. Both enchanted him. "Yes, let's do that. I haven't gone winter tubing in forever. Probably," she mused, "since the last time I went with you. That would have been…your senior year of high school, my junior year."

"I remember," he said softly. And oh, did he ever. That was the winter he'd first seen Rachel as an actual female, and not just one of his favorite buddies. "You stopped being a tomboy that year."

"I stopped *pretending* to be a tomboy that year," she corrected him. "Impressing the boys became critically more important than annoying my parents."

"You were already impressive," he said quietly. "Never doubt that."

She blinked once. Twice. Out of nervousness or surprise, Cole guessed, which proved his point about blinking. He hoped for surprise. He didn't like the idea of making her nervous.

"You're being sweet and sentimental." Lifting her cup to her lips, she swallowed a gulp of her coffee. Cold by now, probably. "So…tubing? Or are we back to shopping?"

"Shopping tomorrow," Cole said firmly. "Today is about fun."

True, yes. But Cole also wanted to finish their conversation from Foster's the other night, and he figured having a little fun together first would help ease the way.

And hell, the distraction would be good. It might even be enough to wipe what Lola had said out of Rachel's mind. He wasn't ready to come clean with her just yet. Not until he understood all of the reason she'd disappeared on him after his accident…and why it had taken her so damn long to return, with or without an invitation.

Yup. He had questions. Perhaps, before the day ended, he'd have some answers.

Exhilaration quickened Rachel's pulse as she jumped on the snow tube and started downhill. Cole had promised fun, and for the past several hours, he had delivered. This was exactly what she'd needed after her draining, confusing and depressing as-all-get-out weekend.

Wind and speed watered her eyes, burned her cheeks. A gurgle of breathless laughter escaped when the tube bounced and swerved, picked up momentum and raced down the hill even faster. She felt like a kid again, like the teenagers she and Cole had reminisced about earlier. Which, naturally, brought to mind his comment.

He'd said, *"You were already impressive. Never doubt that."*

And didn't that just make her stomach twirl? She blinked hard to clear her vision and told herself it was due to the wind, the speed, and not to the fact that back then, her teenage self hadn't yet lost her chance with Cole. Hope still existed, shiny and new.

She came to a halt at the bottom of the hill and yanked herself to the present. Standing, she shielded her eyes from the glare of the sun and watched Cole take the trip she just had. This was the last of their snow-tubing fun for the day. Would they ever come here again, just the two of them? She doubted it.

After all, at this time in a year—assuming that the facts presented before her were actually facts—Cole could very well be a married man. He'd play in the snow with another woman, and a few more years down the road, his children. Heck, he might bring his family to this very spot.

That was fine. Well, it wasn't fine *now,* but if necessary Rachel would adjust and grow into the idea. At some point, surely. Until then, she'd pretend she was fine. That was one thing, thanks to her parents, she'd had plenty of practice with.

Cole's inner tube swerved and slid down the remainder of the hill, and she had her smile ready when he approached. "You were right," she said. "This was a great way to spend the day."

"Yeah? Good. That's real good." He pulled off his gloves and tweaked her nose. A simple touch, barely more than a brush of his fingertips against her skin, but her heart picked up an extra beat. "I don't know about you, but I'm starving. We sort of skipped right by lunch. Feel like grabbing a bite, or do you and Andrew have plans for dinner?"

Tell him now, her inner voice urged. She opened her mouth but couldn't find the words. Later, then. She'd explain the situation regarding Andrew over dinner, or tomorrow, or—again, if the presented facts were reality—after she'd returned to New York. From a distance, where she wouldn't have to see the pity in Cole's eyes. She absolutely wouldn't be able to handle pity.

"Um, no. We didn't make plans for tonight." That was the honest to God truth. "He's likely buried in work at the moment, so I'm free." Also true.

Besides being hungry, she could use the opportunity to ask Cole a few of the questions she hadn't been able to earlier. Silly, she knew, but Lola's certainty that he didn't have a girlfriend had given Rachel hope. For what, exactly, she wasn't sure, because it couldn't be what she'd originally thought. Mary *had* to be real.

Why would Cole make up a woman? Hadn't Margaret Foster just about glowed with pleasure over her son's relationship status? She had. And hadn't Dylan agreed with Cole's explanation about keeping the relationship a secret? That was a yes, as well.

But something was off. And Rachel intended to find out what that something was. Because if she hadn't lost her mind, then the crazy might not be so crazy. The crazy might be real. And then—

"Where to?" Cole asked. "Foster's again?"

"How about your place instead?" she asked. "It will

be quieter there, more relaxed. We can stop by the store and pick up supplies. I'll even cook." Then, testing out her idea, as crazy as it was, she said, "Oh, wow. I'm an idiot. You probably have plans with Mary. I can cook for her, too, if you're ready for us to meet."

"Nice try, Rachel, but not yet," he said easily enough. The muscle in his jaw twitched, so slight she would've missed it if she hadn't been staring at his lips. "She's busy tonight."

"That's too bad. I guess you two probably spent most of the weekend together, right?"

"I worked most of the weekend." Cole put his gloves on again. "But yes, men typically spend their weekends with their girlfriends."

And that was not an answer. Not really. Trying another tack, Rachel said, "How is she liking the gifts so far? You haven't mentioned how your plan is working. I'm curious."

"So far so good. Based on her reactions to the gifts, I'd guess she likes them just fine."

And another non-answer type of answer. "A few details would be nice," she prodded. "What has been her favorite so far?"

"Uh…her favorite?" he asked.

Twitch went that muscle, and darn if Rachel didn't think of what Dylan had said about Cole having a tell. Was this it? Smiling sweetly—and hopefully, innocently—she said, "Yes, you know, her favorite, meaning which gift of those you've given her does she like the most?"

"I haven't asked her that particular question," Cole said after a long pause. "But I'll be sure to when…the correct opportunity presents itself."

"Why don't we call her after dinner and ask her then?"

"You want to talk to her?"

"Sure. Why not?"

"I don't know if that's the best idea," he said. "It might be…somewhat of an uncomfortable situation, you talking to…Mary."

No twitch that time. Hmm. "Never hurts to try, does it?" Rachel spun on her heel without waiting for a response, her mind abuzz with a thousand-and-one insane possibilities. Wishful thinking? Probably. The Cole she knew would never—

A snowball smacked her in the center of her back. All thoughts of Mary fled. Without missing a beat, she knelt down, scraped snow into her gloved hands and formed a solid-but-not-too-firm ball. Raising her arm, she stood, spun again…and didn't see Cole anywhere.

The sneak. He was hiding…somewhere. Waiting for the perfect moment to take her by surprise. Again. She felt her lips curve into a grin. Yes, even with her questions, this fell into the most fun day in a long, long while category.

Squinting against the sun, she turned in a slow circle, looking for denim-covered legs and a red-and-black coat. Several folks were wearing red, more wearing jeans, but none of them were Cole. The wind lifted her hair, tossed it in her eyes. And…slam, another hit. This one on her right arm.

She pivoted, fast. There he was. How had she missed him before? Rolling her shoulder, she aimed for his chest and let her snowball fly. Bull's-eye! His deep, rumbling laugh carried on the wind to her ears, the sound of it causing her own laughter to ring loud and clear.

He had another snowball ready to go. Bringing one

knee up like a pitcher in a baseball game, he wound his arm in an exaggerated motion…she dropped to her knees…and the snowball whizzed over her head. She laughed again, stuck her tongue out at him and crawled across the ground as fast as she could, taking cover near a small cluster of trees. And, knowing Cole wouldn't be able to wait her out, quickly got to work on compiling an arsenal of snowballs.

As she did, she took in her surroundings, trying to deduce which direction he would come toward her from. Ah. *There.* Not too far away, on her left, was another grouping of trees. He'd go around the long way to get there, compile his own arsenal and try another sneak attack. After their many, many snowball wars when they were kids, he should know better.

For whatever reason, Rachel had almost always kicked his butt when they were on opposite teams. Which, she thought with another grin, was why—once he'd figured that out—he would typically team up with her against his brothers.

Cole liked winning. He liked winning against his brothers even more.

Sibling rivalry, she supposed.

A flash of red caught her eye, exactly where she expected he'd be. Pretending to have her attention focused in the opposite direction, Rachel angled herself to the right without losing complete view of her left. He might double back as he got closer.

She shoved two snowballs in each of her jacket pockets, thankful they were deep enough, and grabbed two more. Hmm. He hadn't left the protection of the trees yet. Maybe he was trying to wait her out? A new strategy for him, but he wouldn't succeed.

Impatient, he'd called her…well, okay, he'd used the

word *determined,* but he'd meant impatient. Rachel let out a soft snicker. She was determined, all right—determined to sit right here until he got tired of waiting and came for her.

The seconds ticked by into minutes. How many, she couldn't guess, but long enough for the snow to soak through her jeans and freeze her knees into virtual ice cubes. Repositioning herself into a crouch, she twisted her upper body to the right and stared at the red parka. The red parka that hadn't freaking budged… Oh.

Oh! Why, that rat. He'd almost fooled her. Rachel was ninety-nine percent positive that the coat she glimpsed was minus one Cole Foster, left there as a red herring, while he crept up and took her by surprise. It was, she admitted, an excellent plan.

Moving slowly, and oh-so-carefully, she again twisted her upper body to the right, expecting to see Cole skulking toward her with a sly grin on his handsome face. But…no. Drat it all, where was that man? Giving up any pretense of caution, Rachel pulled herself to a stand, ready to march over to his coat and holler out her surrender, when a snowball crashed into the left side of her head.

And then another hit her shoulder. Before she managed to turn around and volley a few at him—he'd been hiding in *her* clump of trees, directly behind her original position—one more slammed into her lower back. Oh, yes, this was war.

He may have gotten the jump on her, but she could still kick his butt. Silly, silly man, thinking otherwise. For the moment, Rachel let herself take that long, slow slide backward in time, when everything between her and Cole had been effortless and fun and…hopeful.

And wow, did it feel good.

Chapter Eight

When the last snowball on each side had made contact, and Cole's face hurt from smiling so damn hard, he fell to his knees and admitted defeat. Rachel, as always, had proven her snowball-fight expertise and shown him—in no uncertain terms, even—who was boss.

He didn't mind in the least. He sort of liked it, actually.

"You win, Rach," he said. "I am at your mercy."

"Oh, yeah?" She brushed damp hair out of her eyes and dropped down in front of him. "I like the sound of that. In fact," she said with a delicious sort of wink that sent unmanly flutters rippling through his abdomen, "*you* can make dinner tonight."

How could a woman with wet, clumpy hair, face scrubbed clean of cosmetics from exertion and wearing snow-soaked jeans be so ridiculously beautiful? He'd seen her dressed to the hilt in fancy clothes and expensive jewelry, with her makeup applied so that she looked like one of those centerfold models she'd teased him about at Foster's, but damn if he didn't find her more alluring, more sensual, more…everything, just like this.

"You are a strange woman, Rachel Merriday," he said. "I tell you I'm at your mercy, and all you want from me is dinner?"

"I didn't say that was *all* I wanted," she countered, rolling backward and stretching out on the snow. "But it's a good place to start."

He crawled to her side and collapsed, mimicking her position. He was cold and hungry, worn-out to the bone, and thought nothing sounded better than hot food and a hotter shower, but he felt good. Real good. The type of good brought on by being outdoors and playing hard. Kids were used to feeling this way, but Cole hadn't for a long while.

Too long. And he wouldn't hurry this moment away for anything.

"I don't know, darlin'," he said in a teasing, laid-back manner. "You already said you'd do the cooking. Seems to me a woman should live up to her word."

She elbowed him in the side. "What happened to being at my mercy?"

Her words forced his thoughts along a different path, a far steamier one than a simple dinner could provide, but he didn't voice them. Doing so would only bring forth a slew of questions he wasn't prepared to answer. This entire day—snow-tubing and the snowball fight— had been light and carefree. Better, he thought, to keep that momentum going.

He raised his arms above his head, as if he were stretching, and grabbed two handfuls of snow. One quick move had him on his side, facing her. And then… Well, he stopped to take in the sight of her. Eyes closed, body posed in a loose and languid way, breathing slow and even. The impulse to kiss her was strong, unrelenting. It rode through him hard, compelling him to ignore all the reasons why he shouldn't—couldn't—lean in and take her mouth with his.

Screw it. Some things weren't definable. Some things, such as his need for Rachel at that second, couldn't be denied or explained. They just were. So he leaned in closer. And then, a little closer yet. Close enough that he'd be able to count her eyelashes if he wanted.

He didn't. He had other ideas in mind.

And was less than a beat away from bringing those ideas to fruition, from tasting her lips with his, when her breathing stilled and her eyes popped open.

He froze, stared into her eyes, read the surprise there along with another emotion that Cole couldn't identify. Desire, maybe, if he were lucky. Could just as easily have been something else, though. Something that would put an end to…everything he saw between them.

So he did what he'd started off planning to do, he brought his hands up and let the snow sprinkle onto her face. "Got you," he said, hoping his tone had a light enough ring to it. "Couldn't let you fall asleep, not when you promised me a home-cooked meal."

"I can't believe you did that!" She sputtered and blinked, blew snow out of her mouth and sputtered some more. "You, Cole Foster, are nothing but a sore loser."

He smiled, sprinkled a little more snow on her for good measure and stood. "What I am is hungry, wet and cold." Reaching down, he grabbed her hand and helped her up. "Let's go."

"Fine," she huffed. "I'll cook. While I do that, you can get Mary on the phone."

Hell. Now, what in the world was he going to do about that one?

An hour-and-a-half later, after a quick stop at the store, a quicker shower, and a pair of borrowed sweats and a T-shirt—both oversize—Rachel had lived up to her word and put together an easy meal of tomato soup and grilled cheese with ham sandwiches. Now, Cole was finishing clean-up duty, which was the deal they'd settled on: she'd cook, he'd clean.

Up until two years ago, Cole had lived in the small apartment above Foster's Pub and Grill. When he bought this place—a two-bedroom log cabin on the outskirts of Steamboat Springs—Haley had claimed the apartment as hers.

During Rachel's visit last year, Cole had still been in the process of renovating the kitchen. With his attention otherwise occupied, Rachel looked over the changes he'd made. The room, while not overly large, had an airy, open ambience that she liked. He'd chosen sturdy oak cabinets and hardwood floors, cinnamon-and-cream pebbled granite countertops and what appeared to be straight-from-Grandma's-kitchen white appliances.

Navy blue, deep green and splashes of russet were found in the dishtowels, curtains and throw rugs. The walls, unfortunately, were mostly bare and were painted the standard off-white. If she lived here, she'd add plants and pictures and maybe paint the walls an actual shade.

Still, all in all, the kitchen spoke to her. It was, she thought, a room to relax and chat in after a long day. She could see herself here, almost too well.

More than that, she could see herself with the man.

He was a stellar specimen of the male species, with his chocolate-brown eyes and thick, black-as-coal hair, and a strong body that looked damn awesome in a pair of jeans. She loved his laugh, too. That rumbling, warm, full-of-life laugh of his made her feel…secure, in some way.

Rubbing her hand across her face, she tried to dispel her tiredness and her confusion. Naturally, neither occurred. She returned to that moment when she was lying in the snow, relaxed and content, happy with how the day had progressed. All at once, a telltale tingle had whispered along her skin, raising goose bumps and forcing her eyes open.

And there he was. Right there, so very close.

She'd have sworn he was going to kiss her. Dear Lord, she'd *wanted* him to kiss her. Instead, she'd gotten snow in her face, and that deep, throaty laugh. In the snap of a finger, the moment ended, and they were—once again— nothing more than friends having fun.

Rachel pushed out a breath, and with it, the memory.

"You're awfully quiet," Cole said, hanging the dishtowel over the sink.

"Just thinking," she replied with a yawn.

"About?" He returned to the table, sat down and cradled his arms behind his head. The action caused his shirt to tighten around his chest, accentuating his lean, muscular angles, and it was all Rachel could do not to stare.

Or imagine ripping that shirt clean off of him and leading him toward the bedroom. Oh, God. Not what she should be thinking about.

"Tomorrow, and the gifts we still need to get," she said, forcing her thoughts into safer territory. She'd asked him, once again, to phone Mary before dinner.

He'd refused. Stated that the conversation would be "uncomfortable" and "awkward," and he'd prefer if Rachel stuck to their original agreement. Which, of course, meant zero contact with Mary until after the proposal.

Fair enough, she supposed. Perfectly reasonable, even, since she had agreed to those ridiculous terms. Somehow, though, for reasons she couldn't fully explain, her instincts remained on high alert. She really, really wanted to trust in those instincts.

"I'm sure we'll be able to get through them quick enough," Cole said. "If nothing else, we can fall back on the vacuum-cleaner idea."

She snorted. "You do that. While you're at it, why not buy Mary another flashlight, as well? Maybe some batteries to go with it, and hey…I know! How about a sewing machine so she can mend all your loose buttons and torn shirts?"

His mouth split into the goofy grin she adored. "Two flashlights are overkill. She doesn't sew, but hey, nice idea. The batteries could work, but isn't that a bit…I don't know, cheap to give them as a separate gift?"

"I was teasing, which you know." Her instincts buzzed harder. "What type of music does Mary like? What's her favorite movie, favorite author? Does she enjoy cooking? Does she wear jewelry? Is she a dog or a cat person?"

"Whoa there, Rach. That's an awful lot of questions."

"If you're considering *marrying* her, then you should know the answers."

"Of course I know the answers!" Cole sat up straight and shifted in his seat. "But would you rather be given a CD of your favorite type of music or something unexpected, something that you'd never think of buying yourself in a million years?" He shrugged. "I think the unexpected is more romantic than the obvious."

He had her there. Damn him. She wasn't about to let on to that though. "Yes," she said with a sniff, "I would never, in a million years, buy myself a flashlight."

"You would, but not for the same reason *I* bought that particular flashlight."

And that made zero sense. She regarded him silently, trying to decide what he was up to. Even if Mary existed, even if Rachel had lost her mind, he was up to something. He *had* to be up to something. She had to figure out what.

"Do you have some paper and a pen around here somewhere?" she asked. "I'd like to write a list, see everything we've already bought in print. Maybe then, I'll be able to align my thinking with yours, so we're… um…on the same page."

One eyebrow quirked in curious amusement, but he didn't argue. He left the room, returning a minute later with the requested items, which he dropped on the table in front of her.

"Thank you," she said as she flipped open the spiral-bound notebook.

"Welcome." Rather than retaking the seat he'd vacated on the other side of the table, he sat in the chair next to her. So close, she could feel the heat of his body. "I'm really okay with the roaming and talking method, Rach. We don't need a list for tomorrow."

"Shh. Maybe you don't, but I do."

On a clean page, she numbered from one to ten along the left margin, filling in the top five lines with the gifts they'd already purchased. Next to each item, she then

wrote the reason—as she understood it—for buying that
particular gift.

When she was done, she had:

Snow Globe—Representation of when/how they
met (outside in the winter)
Photo Album—To put pictures of their journey so
far (they met as children)
Camera—To create more memories with
My Perfume—Because he likes the scent/doesn't
know what brand she wears
Flashlight—No freaking idea why or what he's
thinking

She read the list once, twice. Squeezed her eyes shut
for a millisecond and then read the list again. Her mind
replayed every last thing that had happened since she'd
arrived in Steamboat Springs, beginning from the moment she and Andrew had stepped into the Beanery.

Cole's unexpected announcement that he had a girlfriend. His crazy plea for Rachel's help in wooing Cupcake, a woman whose first name he refused to share.
How his friendship with Rachel had prepared him for
this relationship because the two women shared similar
pasts, similar temperaments, similar…barriers.

What else? Margaret Foster's obvious pleasure when
she spoke of Cole's falling in love weighed against Lola's
certainty that he didn't have a girlfriend. *The vase.* Cole's
words about Rachel's eyes, how she'd then deemed the
vase a romantic gift because of that sentiment, followed
by his intense reaction to that.

One by one, each moment, each conversation, each
time he'd sidestep one of her questions, each odd look
and muffled laugh…all of it roared through her head,

along with images of his teasing smile, their absurd winter picnic at the playground, the way he'd... Oh.

She drew in a sharp breath and read the list for the fourth time.

Why, the sneaky devil. The snow globe represented how he and Cupcake met, did it? Well, Rachel had met Cole in the winter, outside, in the school playground. And no man in his right mind bought the woman he loved another woman's favorite perfume. *Rachel's* scent.

Swallowing past the lump in her throat, she tried to find the weak threads holding her conclusion together, tried to convince herself that this *couldn't* be the case. Could *she* be Mary? Could she be... If Cole loved *her,* wanted to romance *her,* why wouldn't he just tell her? Why would he go to such extremes to get her attention? Was he trying to make her jealous, or...?

"Andrew," she whispered. She hadn't told Cole about Andrew until...oh, a week or so before arriving in Steamboat Springs, when the decision had become final. Why had she waited? Because...she hadn't yet decided if her relationship with Andrew was important enough to mention? Or because she was still hanging on to hope she didn't know she had?

Both, probably.

"Andrew? Did you need to call him?" Cole asked, interrupting the forward motion of her thoughts. "Go ahead, Rach. I'll...go put your clothes in the dryer. Give you a little privacy."

She nodded faintly as he stepped away from the table, piecing together what she *hoped* to be true with what she actually knew. She could be wrong. This could still be nothing more than wishful thinking. But if she weren't... was it even remotely possible that Cole had created a fake girlfriend out of jealousy? To accomplish what, exactly?

He'd said he wanted to "woo" Mary. That he needed Rachel's help. She'd seen love in his eyes, for crying out loud. But…well, in addition to all the wonderful and sweet comments he'd made about his Cupcake, he'd also expressed *serious* concerns. Concerns he wanted to talk over with Rachel, so that she could help him see those "issues" in the right light.

Because women were a mystery.

She dropped her gaze to the list again, read what she'd written, considered and analyzed the entire situation, everything she knew about Cole and their shared past, and tried to determine where she should go from here. Ask him? Just flat-out tell him her suspicions?

The thought held merit. But. What. If. She. Were. Wrong?

Could she handle *that* outcome? Probably, yes, although it would be a humiliating and miserable experience. A shudder rippled through her at the thought, at the very image of how that conversation would turn out. The sympathy and shock and…pity. Hell, if she was totally off base, she'd come off as a love-struck loon. A crazy person. Ugh.

But…if she were right, why stop now?

A glimmer of an idea set in. She could turn the tables, play a bit of Cole's game on him, lead him down the same convoluted path he'd been leading her. Discuss those serious concerns of his under the guise he'd created, which frankly, might allow them to be one hundred percent honest with each other, about their past and the decisions they'd each made. Yes, she thought, as whacked as the idea was, that also held merit.

She needed confirmation, though. She needed to

know if what she thought was going on was, in fact, what was really going on. Only then could she make a decision of how to proceed.

But oh, if Cole had done this instead of just talking to her, instead of being open and honest and admitting his feelings—those concerns of his—then a little payback was definitely in order. She loved him, yes. She knew that now, without doubt or question.

Unfair, though, playing with her emotions. Wrong, too. And if he did love her, if that hope turned into reality, then she needed to know he wouldn't do something like this again. She needed to know that he trusted her, trusted *them,* and would turn to her instead of relying on deception as a means to an end.

Of course, that didn't rule out the fun-factor in teaching him that particular lesson. A small, quiet laugh slipped out. Oh, she'd have fun, all right. In spades.

Confirmation first, though. And, thanks to Dylan and his illuminating insight on the subject of tells, Rachel thought she knew exactly how to get it.

The next morning, Rachel spent close to an hour on the phone with her mother, attempting to convince her that, no, she still had not heard from her father. Atypical behavior for Lawrence Merriday? Yes. But also not a complete aberration.

Rachel's father was the president and chairman-of-the-board for a multi-million dollar paper manufacturing company that *his* great-grandfather had started eons ago as a small business with only a handful of employees. If there were any knots requiring untangling at MPM—Merriday Paper Manufacturing—her father would see to that before focusing on this latest battle with her mother.

Then, though, he'd be full-in. That was when Rachel figured he'd contact her.

Candace knew this as well as Rachel did, but for whatever reason, seemed more distracted, more depressed, than usual by whatever was going on between them. She was also behaving atypically, not that Rachel said that to her in so many words.

But it did cause her concern. Enough concern that when Candace claimed she'd had second thoughts and had decided to stay in New York for the holidays, Rachel talked her into coming to Steamboat Springs. It took some doing, which was…yep, also atypical, but finally her mother agreed. She would be here on Thursday afternoon.

Then, Rachel hurriedly went through her closet, filling two large boxes with an assortment of designer clothes for Haley. She had less than two hours before she met with Cole to finish their oh-so-fun shopping trip, and chatting with his sister beforehand was essential.

The clothes served as an excellent excuse to drop by.

If she were there at the right time, she might bump into Reid. Oh, seeing any of the Fosters would be a pleasure, but Reid and Haley were the only two who could give her the confirmation she wanted. After all, she'd been told clear as day what their "tells" were.

She didn't call before heading to Foster's Pub and Grill, deciding to go with a surprise visit. Hey, surprise had worked well for Cole, so why not? Once there, she went directly to the back entrance since the restaurant hadn't yet opened for the day. She had to put the boxes down in order to knock, and while she waited, she went over her plan of attack.

Throughout the long, sleepless hours the night before, Rachel had given considerable thought to the forthcoming conversation. She couldn't outright share her suspicions with Haley, or with Reid if he were around, because as much as they might like her, the Fosters were tight. What Haley and Reid knew, Rachel felt sure Cole would know before she'd made it back to her car. Also, she couldn't rule out the possibility that she was wrong.

Being wrong was one thing. Letting Cole in on her feelings if he loved another woman? No. She couldn't—wouldn't—go there.

Rachel knocked again, a little harder this time. What if she was right, but Cole hadn't shared any of this with Haley and Reid? There wouldn't be any tells then, regardless of what questions Rachel asked, because they wouldn't be in on the scheme.

Oh, hell. Why hadn't she thought of that before?

Except…that seemed unlikely. Either Mary existed or Cole had told his family what he was really up to. Otherwise, why would his mother have said what she did? That made sense.

Rachel was readying herself to knock one more time when the door swung open by a smiling Paul Foster. His hair had grayed some since she last saw him, but he looked fit and healthy and very much like a man happy with his lot in life.

"Well, hello there, Rachel. I heard you were in town." He shot an inquisitive look toward the boxes before opening the door wider. "Come in, have some coffee. Cole isn't here, though."

She returned his smile. "Actually, I'm here to make Haley's day."

"Well, I'm sure she'll be pleased to hear that," Paul said. He bent over and picked up the topmost box. "She's in the office gathering some stuff to take with her to the sporting goods store, since she'll be helping out there today."

Right. While Cole took off with Rachel. Good thing she'd gotten here when she did. "Glad I caught her before she left," Rachel said, gathering the remaining box in her arms. "Is…uh…Reid here by chance?"

"He was earlier," Paul said, leading the way toward the office, "but left about thirty minutes or so ago, I'd reckon. Were you planning on making his day, too?"

Rachel laughed. "I just wanted to say hi. He's the only Foster left I haven't seen."

"Gotcha. Well, I'm sure you'll be in the same place at the same time soon enough." Paul paused in front of an open door to a large room. Inside, Haley sat at one of three desks, busily sorting a stack of files. He winked at Rachel. In a booming voice, he said, "Look who is here to make your day, Haley!"

The woman jumped, brought her hand to her chest. "Dad! You know how much I hate when you do that. I swear, you stay up late thinking of ways to—" Her eyes landed on Rachel. A wide smile appeared. "Rachel! What are you doing here? Did we have plans I forgot about?"

Paul entered the office and deposited the box he carried at Haley's feet. "I'll leave you two alone," he said, retreating to the doorway. "Coffee is in the kitchen, if you'd like some."

He was gone before Rachel could reply. More atypical behavior. In the past, Paul would always take a few minutes to chat, ask what she'd been up to, about her parents. Of course, he was working now. Perhaps he'd been in the middle of something he needed to get back to.

Brushing the thoughts aside, Rachel walked to Haley's desk, put her box on top of the other. "You didn't forget anything. I cleaned out my closet this morning, so figured why keep you waiting for a new wardrobe when I could bring the clothes to you?"

"Yeah?" She looked from Rachel to the boxes. "Can I…?"

"Go for it."

Haley tore into the boxes, one after another, pulling out and holding each item up to her long and lanky frame. Rachel stood by and watched, offering appropriate comments at the appropriate times, itchy with nerves for what came next.

The entire process took no more than twenty minutes, but when Haley finally collapsed in her chair, Rachel felt as if an entire twenty-four hours had passed. She pulled one of the other desk chairs over to sit in, smiled and said, "I take it you're pleased with my choices?"

"Are you kidding? I'm ecstatic. Say what you will about your mother, but she has fantastic taste in clothes." Haley reverently slid her hand over each box. "And you know I'm eternally grateful for your generosity, but… um…are you nuts? Why would you give away such beautiful stuff? They all look brand-new, as if you've never worn them."

Rachel shrugged. The truth was, she hadn't worn most of what she'd given Haley. "Half of what's there aren't this year's styles," Rachel offered as an excuse, though she never cared a bit about that, "and have been hanging in my closet here since last year. The rest aren't my style, but I thought they would suit you. If you don't want them, I'm sure—"

"Oh, right. Like I'm going to turn away gorgeous clothes that I could never afford to buy on my own. I don't think so." Haley reached over, squeezed Rachel's hand. "Thank you."

"You're welcome," Rachel said simply. Despite her real motive for bringing the clothes this morning, she loved how happy they made Haley. "Enjoy."

"Trust me, I will." She glanced at the clock. "Do you want a cup of coffee? I might be able to snag us a few Christmas cookies, if Mom isn't looking."

"I'm good." Rachel paused, brought the words to mind she intended to say, and hoped for the best. "Did you know I've been helping Cole choose gifts for his girlfriend?"

"He mentioned something along those lines," Haley affirmed, her fingers entwined on the surface of the desk. "I know he was thrilled you agreed to...help."

"Well, how could I say no? I mean, I've never seen him this excited, this...focused on making another woman happy." Rachel leaned forward and lowered her voice, as if sharing a secret. "I had no idea that Cole had such a romantic side to his personality."

Green eyes widened innocently. Real or fake? "I know! Who'd have guessed?"

"Exactly! He's always been so, I don't know, laid-back about women." Tucking a strand of hair behind her ear, Rachel expelled a dramatic sigh. "But...he's really counting on me. I'm afraid I'm going to let him down."

"In what way?"

"Well, we're supposed to finish buying gifts today, for Mary—that's what we've decided to call her, since Cole won't tell me her real name—and so far, some of his choices have been...questionable, I guess you'd say."

"Oh, I'm sure Cole knows precisely what he's doing." Haley squeezed Rachel's hand again. "Don't worry too much. I doubt you'll let him down."

"He bought her a flashlight, and seems set on getting her a vacuum cleaner." With a groan, Rachel fell against the back of her chair. "His heart is in the right place, but his choices aren't… Well, I don't see how they're going to win her over. I need your help, Haley."

"I'm not sure…that is, what type of help?"

"You know Mary, right?"

"Yes. Of course I…know her."

"Then you tell me, will a vacuum cleaner and a flashlight win her over?"

"I'm not really supposed to talk about this with you," Haley said carefully. "Cole specifically asked each of us in the family to…stay clear of this topic."

"Oh, come on. Really? Isn't that a little ridiculous?" Haley didn't respond, just kept her expression neutral. "Look, I'm not trying to weasel any identifying information out of you. A promise is a promise, and I respect that." She gave Haley what she hoped was a beseeching look, softened her voice and said, "All I need is a little help in ascertaining I do right by Cole."

Ten seconds, then twenty ticked by before Haley sighed. "I can't say a lot," she warned, "but I'll help if I can. What do you want to know?"

Jackpot. Pleased, Rachel nodded her thanks, knowing she had to start off slow and warm into the questions she really wanted answered. "Well, for starters, it would be hugely helpful if I understood more about their relationship. Maybe, without going into any specific details about who Mary is, you could tell me what they're like together as a couple?"

"Oh, they're one of those couples that truly fit each other. We…that is, everyone in the family…have known so forever," Haley all but gushed. "For years, Cole would deny that he had feelings for…Mary, but we all knew he did."

"So they complement each other? Is that what you mean?"

Rather than replying verbally, Haley nodded.

Okay. Moving on. "I would guess, then, that their backgrounds are the same? Mary grew up here in Steamboat Springs, went to the same schools as you guys, all that stuff?"

"Um, well." Haley's gaze shifted to the right. "She… How is this helpful?"

"If I have a better feeling for the type of person Mary is, then I'll be more capable of aiming Cole in the right direction. A lot of who we are is often dictated by our backgrounds."

Huh. Sounded plausible to Rachel, anyway.

"Okay, yeah. I see what you're getting at." Haley flipped her hair forward, started twirling a chunk of it with her finger. Aha! "Um, yes. We've known her for… well, forever."

"Hmm," Rachel murmured, as if absorbing the information. "That's good to know. What about her career? Does she work in the tourist industry here in Steamboat?" And then, before Haley could put up a fuss, said, "What careers we choose also speak to who we are."

"She's…ah…sort of in between jobs at the moment."

"A lot of folks are out of work these days," Rachel said in a compassionate tone. "What did she do before she was 'in between jobs'?"

More twirling. Haley swallowed and shrugged. "She's done a lot of different things. I really can't remember every job she's ever had."

"Nothing at all?"

"No. Nothing at all." If she wrapped that lock of hair any tighter around her finger, she'd soon have a bald spot. "Sorry."

Rachel groaned again, louder than before, all for Haley's benefit. "Well, gee. I don't know what to do, then. Poor Mary. I really hope she likes clean carpets."

"Don't let him buy the vacuum cleaner," Haley said, sounding more like herself. Returning her gaze to Rachel, finally, she laughed. "Seriously, I wouldn't worry about this. You're a woman. You know what women consider romantic. Go with your gut, Rachel."

"I think that's the best advice I've had all day," Rachel said with a huge smile. She'd had a few other questions but was afraid to push her luck. Besides which, supposing Dylan's assessment about Haley and her tells were correct, Rachel had enough. *More* than enough. "You're absolutely right. I'll just…trust my instincts."

"So, no more questions?" Haley asked with a relieved ring in her voice. "We're done?"

"Nope, no more. And yes, we're done." Crossing her fingers over her heart, she said, "Don't stress about any of this, I won't say a word to Cole. Promise."

"Cool. I won't, either."

They talked for another fifteen minutes, steering clear of the subject of Cole and Mary, focusing instead on normal girl chat. Rachel truly did adore Haley, and she enjoyed the time she spent with her but was equally as anxious to put the next part of her plan in motion.

When Rachel left, she was caught somewhere in the middle of shock, happiness and irritation. The happy would rule out, eventually, but not until she gave Cole a little of what he'd given her. He wanted to play games, did he? Well, she had a few moves of her own. Moves, she was sure, he wouldn't see coming. Moves that would knock the breath from his lungs.

She'd have him begging for mercy soon enough, just like yesterday with the snowball fight. This time, though, the game wouldn't end with snow being tossed in her face. This time, she'd get that kiss…and if she—*they*—were very lucky, a whole hell of a lot more.

But all of that started with teaching Mr. Cole Foster a lesson he'd never forget.

Chapter Nine

Cole had had about enough of the crowds, the overly warm stores, the way-too-eager salespeople and the nonstop noise of holiday music. Not to mention how damn long it had taken them to find a parking space. Without a doubt, he disliked everything about large, enclosed spaces, which made being at the mall almost unbearable. Rachel had insisted, though, stating they'd already visited every other store in Steamboat Springs, so it was beyond time to expand their options. He'd reluctantly agreed. Now, he wished he hadn't. Mostly due to the establishment they now stood in.

"I'm not sure this is the way to go," Cole said, fingering the silky red negligee she'd thrust into his hands. "Don't women hate gifts like this? I mean, won't she view this as more for my benefit than hers?"

"Only if you're the typical lughead, which you're not." Reclaiming the negligee, Rachel swung the garment in front of her as if it were a pendulum. "Imagine Mary wearing this, Cole. You said she was gorgeous, right? How would she look in this?"

He swallowed, hard, and tried to do exactly the opposite. Visualizing Rachel in that bit of fabric would not be a good idea. Especially in public. "She'd be… irresistible."

"Good." Rachel nodded, as if pleased with his description. "Now, consider how you would feel seeing her in this, and then consider all the different methods you could use to make *her* feel incredible. If you make this negligee all about her, and the pleasure you can give her, then trust me, she'll be a very happy and satisfied woman."

Cole tugged at the collar of his shirt, which had inexplicably seemed to tighten the longer Rachel talked. Beads of perspiration dotted his forehead and the back of his neck, adding to his distress. "It's a little hot in here, isn't it?"

"Is it? I hadn't noticed." Smiling indulgently, she plastered the negligee tight against her body. "Maybe I should slip into the dressing room and try this on. Give you an actual picture to work with, rather than guessing how the negligee looks on a woman's shape. Would that help?"

"No!" he all but yelled. Several shoppers turned to stare. He ignored them and worked to regain control of his libido. "That isn't necessary. I…I get what you're saying. Even so," he said in a voice as strained as his jeans were becoming, "I'd rather go in a different direction."

Disappointment flickered over her features. "Are you sure?"

"Yes." He loosened his knees and bent them slightly, not enough to call notice to the action, but enough to alleviate his discomfort. An unsuccessful attempt, as it turned out. Where the hell was a cold shower when a man needed one? "I'm absolutely positive."

"I suppose you know what's best." She went to put the blasted negligee back where she'd gotten it from, stopped and faced him again. "Actually," she said slowly, with a downright wicked gleam darkening her eyes, "I *am* going to try this on."

"No, Rach," he repeated. "There isn't any reason to, since I'm not buying it. Mary wouldn't…I…" He gulped for air, unable to conceive of anything coherent to say. "Don't."

"Oh, not on your account, silly. For me." Her smile brightened and her lashes fluttered into a sleepy sort of blink. "For the man in my life. If I like how this looks on me, that is." She held the silky negligee against her body again. "If *you* were that man, and I walked down the stairs wearing this, with a few Christmas bows placed in strategic positions, would you consider—"

"I'll buy the negligee!" Cole interrupted her, fast, before she could continue on with that tormenting train of thought. God help him, but the idea of Andrew seeing the woman he loved in that slinky, sexy, revealing get-up had sent a stabbing pain directly between his eyes.

Nope. No way, no how was she buying that with Andrew in mind when Cole was with her. Not if he could stop her.

"I thought you said you wanted to go in a different direction?"

"I did, but now that I've had a moment to reconsider, I think you're right on the money." He snatched the red lingerie from Rachel's grip. A tremor of relief rolled down his backbone. "Let me just buy this and we'll get out of here."

Tipping her head, she stared at him for a second. Probably wondering what had gotten into him. "Not so fast, buddy," she said. "I still want to browse, see if I can find something else. I'll do that while you're waiting in line."

Great. Knowing his recent luck, she'd lock on to an even more revealing slip of silk and insist on trying the darn thing on.

Desperation crept through him. He had to get them out of here. As fast as possible. Before…well, before he listened to his sister and resorted to kidnapping.

"Actually, I'd rather we move on as soon as I buy this," he said, thinking on his feet. "We have a few more items to get, and remember, we're supposed to be finishing *my* shopping."

"Right." She huffed out an irritated breath. "Okay, then, since you're in such a hurry, I'll wait out front." She gave a last, lingering glance at the selection of lingerie nearest her. "Maybe if we hurry this along, we can come back later."

With a threat like that, he'd go out of his way to ascertain they did not hurry anything along. What he said, though, was, "Sure. No problem. Whatever you want."

His answer seemed to mollify her, thank goodness. She came to him, stood on her tiptoes and gave him a sweet, small kiss on his cheek. It was disgustingly chaste.

"Thank you, Cole. I want this Christmas to be something truly special for my man." Then, with a toss of her long, blond, silkier-than-the-negligee hair over her shoulders, she raised her lips to his ear and whispered, "And hot. As hot and delicious as I can make it."

She retreated an inch or so, winked and strutted—yes, strutted was the appropriate term—toward the front of the store, her hips sashaying back and forth. Hot, she'd said. And delicious. What did that even mean?

Dammit. After yesterday, he'd almost believed his plan was succeeding. Now, he had to wonder if he'd been fooling himself. Or had something changed?

He stepped forward as the line moved, lost in thought. Perhaps all of this, every last bit of it, was indeed a massive mistake, just as Reid had said. While Cole pretended to be in love with someone else, Rachel might very well be falling in love with Andrew.

Due to the charade? *In spite of?*

Cole shook his head, frustrated. Should he consider bowing out? The deception, which had started off harmlessly enough, was already becoming an unmanageable beast. Every single time Rachel asked a question about "Mary," he had to lie outright, evade the question or find a creatively honest answer. Which, he admitted, was pretty much the same as a lie.

He didn't like lying in general. He despised lying to Rachel.

On the other side of the dilemma, he wasn't ready to give up, even if he *should.* Though, if Rachel actually said the words "I love Andrew," that would be a different matter entirely.

The stabbing sensation relocated to his heart. Yup, kidnapping Rachel and whisking her somewhere—anywhere—far, far away was becoming more appealing by the second.

When Cole reached the front of the line, he handed the negligee to the cashier and waited while she rung it up. He pushed his credit card through the digital reader, declined the offered gift wrapping and finally, followed in Rachel's footsteps.

Soon, he promised himself, he'd delve into the conversation they needed to have. He should have yesterday, had planned to, but they'd had such a great day—natural and fun, the way they used to be together—that he hadn't wanted to end something so positive on a sour note.

Or maybe he was just afraid.

About three feet from exiting the store, a saleswoman tapped him on his arm. Thinking he'd forgotten his wallet at the counter, he reached for his back pocket as he stopped. "Yes?"

"Excuse me, but is your name Cole?" she asked.

"Yeah." His wallet was safe and sound, right where it should be. "That's me."

"Your friend asked me to get you." She nodded toward the rear of the store. "She found something she would like your opinion on."

"Lovely," he muttered, heading in that direction. Cole felt pretty dang sure that whatever Rachel wanted to show him in this store, he'd rather not see. Not with the words *hot* and *delicious* attached to Andrew scorched in his brain.

But he couldn't very well leave her here, now could he?

Sighing, Cole weaved his way around other shoppers—mostly men appearing as confused and out of place as he felt—and kept an eye out for Rachel's blond hair and the holly-green sweater she was wearing.

He saw neither.

When he could go no farther, he located an empty section of wall and leaned against it to wait. She'd find him, he knew, when she was good and ready. Until then, he'd try to ignore the thongs, panties, bras and various other unmentionables cluttering the space around him.

Every one of them put a picture of a half-naked Rachel in his head. Pleasurable, yes. Desirable, exceptionally so. Images he'd likely think of later, when he was alone at home.

But not here. Not when he had to keep his wits about him.

"Cole," Rachel called in a low voice from somewhere to his left. "Where are you?"

He jerked his head to the left, didn't see her. "I'm standing amidst a sea of women's under…things, exactly where the saleswoman directed me," he said somewhat sheepishly, feeling about as foolish as he ever had. "Where are *you?*"

"Over here," she said. "At the dressing rooms."

Oh, crap. Along the left-side wall, on the other side of the shelves and shelves of panties he stood by, were five individual dressing…stalls, Cole guessed they'd be called, and yep, there was Rachel's blond-haired head peeking out from one of them.

"You want me to come there? I don't know, Rach—"

"Just get over here already, will you? Geez."

People were staring again, looking from her to him, most of whom had amused expressions decorating their faces. Yeah. This was fun.

Cole hesitated, caught between two impenetrable barriers. Hell, yes, he wanted to see Rachel in whatever slinky bit of something she likely had on. How could he not? But dammit, she'd all but said her plan was to seduce Andrew for Christmas. With Christmas bows placed in strategic positions, no less. Put the two together, and it was enough to drive a man insane.

Glowering, Cole pushed off the wall and started forward. He could handle this. He'd dealt with far worse, hadn't he? His accident, for one. The surgeries and the seemingly endless rehab that followed. Painful and miserable experiences that had altered Cole forever.

Right. Getting through the next few minutes couldn't possibly be more excruciating.

He stopped at the dressing room door, which was closed again, inhaled a deep, fortifying breath and tapped lightly. Rachel opened the door and yanked him inside before he knew what was happening. Hell, again. Was he even allowed to be in here with her? Surely, store policy—

And then, he quit thinking altogether.

"What do you think?" she asked, turning in a circle. "Would this set a man on fire?"

"Um." He coughed, closed his eyes. Didn't work. He could still see her, the image burned into his brain for all eternity. "I…ah…probably shouldn't be in here."

"Oh, it's fine," she said breezily.

"Still…this…um…" He mentally recited the alphabet. Yup, all the letters were there. Apparently, he'd only lost the ability to use those letters to form actual words. Backing up, he shoved his body against the door. And kept his eyes shut. "Not a good idea," he muttered.

"Why, Cole Foster, are you embarrassed?" A slow, sultry laugh whispered through the air. She brushed his jaw with her fingers. "Don't be silly. You can't give me your opinion if you don't look. And I really, really need your opinion."

"You…ah…" God help him, if he opened his eyes, he was going to do something he should not do. "Haley," he croaked. "Call Haley. She…er, loves clothes."

"But you're here now, and you're my best friend." Another deep-throated laugh that sent his already out-of-control libido into another hemisphere. "*Forever* friends, right?"

Cole swallowed, nodded. He was behaving like an idiot, he knew, but didn't see a way around that fact at this particular moment. Rachel was involved with another man. The only available course of action was to make his escape before he gave in to his baser instincts.

Reaching behind him, he located and twisted the doorknob, cracked open the door and slithered to the side. He'd just...well, he'd wait outside the store. By the time Rachel reappeared—spitting mad, probably—he'd have regained his control.

Almost as soon as the thought had processed, a warm body—*Rachel's* warm body—was pressed against his. He heard her hands make contact with the door, heard the door click shut again. In a very different circumstance, this could be every man's fantasy coming true.

Not in this scenario, unfortunately.

"Oh, no, you don't," she said, her mouth at his ear, her breath hot against his neck. "With all of the help I've given you, you can't do this one miniscule thing for me?"

"I... Andrew wouldn't like it," he said, though he couldn't care less about that. He needed an excuse and that seemed a rather good one. "He has that jealous nature."

"Andrew no longer has any issues with our friendship," she said, her mouth still dangerously close to his. "I told you that, remember?"

"Uh." Great. He was back to speaking in grunts.

"Sweet, though, how you thought of him." The warmth of her body, her breath, the touch of her mouth on his skin, disappeared as she retreated a few inches. "But he understands our...relationship quite well. Perfectly, in fact."

"*I* wouldn't like it," Cole said, hanging on to the only rope he had. "If you were my girlfriend, that is. Showing yourself off to another man. No. No, Rach."

"But you're not Andrew, now, are you?" She paused,

sighed. "Open your eyes, give me your opinion, and we can get out of here."

Nope. There wasn't any escaping this.

Cole breathed in through his nose, visualized standing in an ice-cold shower, gripped his hands into fists and…opened his eyes.

Again, she swirled in a circle. "What do you think?"

Blood rushed to his head. He pressed himself harder against the door.

"You're beautiful, Rach," he said quietly, unable to tear his gaze away from her.

What she'd chosen to model wasn't a negligee, but a long, sheer, sleeveless gown in a rich, satiny midnight blue. The neckline plunged almost to her belly button, giving him a tantalizing glimpse of luscious, creamy skin that reminded him of moonlight.

It was the back, though, that stopped Cole's heart. Because, well, there wasn't a back. Technically speaking, anyway. Nothing existed but bare skin from the arch of her neck, down the length of her spine, all the way to the swell of her hips and the indent of her lower back.

Bare. Deliciously, exquisitely bare.

Mine, his primal self declared. *She. Is. Mine.*

Seemingly unaware of the hunger roaring through Cole's blood, the heat and the desire and the *need* awakening every nerve in his body, or of how close she stood to a man on the edge, she ruffled her hair with her fingers, so that it billowed and fell around her face in a soft, glorious tumble, fluttered her lashes and struck a centerfold pose.

"Will this get the job done?" she asked. "Or should I look for something else?"

The gown, from the color to the fabric to the way it slipped and slid over her body, was made for Rachel.

Only for Rachel. He couldn't say otherwise, couldn't state that she should find something else when *nothing* else would be as perfect.

Jealousy replaced hunger. Anger at himself, at the entire situation—a situation he created—overtook desire. There was only one answer he could give her, in spite of both realities.

"Buy it, Rach," he said in a near growl. "Andrew will be on his knees."

She smiled broadly, brightly, catapulted her body toward him so that he had no choice but to wrap his arms around her. "Thank you for being such a wonderful friend," she said. "I just adore you, Cole. So very much. Why, I don't know what I'd do without you."

"You'll never have to find out," he said. "I'll always be here for you."

He breathed in her scent, that spicy, fruity fragrance that was—to him—all Rachel, and fought the nearly overwhelming urge to tease his fingers beneath the rich, midnight-blue fabric, to stroke her moonlight skin. To caress and touch and pleasure her until she moaned *his* name.

It would be so easy. The heat of her body pushed against his, the softness of her hair feathering along his jaw, the nearness of her lips and the sound of her breathing…everything about the moment, everything about *her* beckoned him, pleaded with him to *act*.

But he couldn't, wouldn't. Unless, "Are you in love, sweetheart?"

"Yes," she said simply, instantly. "I am."

He expelled a rough, ragged sigh and kissed the top of her head. Pulled her close for another heart-wrenching second, and then dropped his hold on her—figuratively and literally.

The gig was up.

* * *

Thursday morning, Rachel spent several hours readying the house for her mother's arrival that afternoon. She could've phoned the housekeeping service her parents employed, but she actually liked doing domestic chores. Well, not *all* domestic chores.

She could go another lifetime without cleaning a toilet, thank you very much.

However, she did enjoy the simple routine of dusting or vacuuming or folding laundry. The sort of busy work that allowed her mind to wander, consider and solve problems, and—as was the case today—fantasize about a certain sexy man.

And what might have happened in that dressing room on Tuesday if they weren't involved in a crazy game of pretend. Nuts. All of it.

Rachel smoothed the sheets on her mother's bed before pulling up the comforter. Truth be told, her skin still tingled from the intense, hungry look Cole had seared her with. The heat in his eyes had set her ablaze, from head to toe and everywhere in between. He'd wanted her, she knew, as much as she'd wanted him. Powerful knowledge, that.

Enough power that she'd almost let her guard down, almost told him the truth—that Andrew was no longer in the picture—had never *really* been in the picture, that she loved Cole, that she'd figured out his charade and had turned the tables on him.

But every out she gave him to come clean on his own, he didn't take. She wanted, maybe needed, for Cole to break the silence first, to tell her that she was Mary and that he loved her. *Rachel.* Whether that was romantic, silly, prideful or all three, she didn't know.

Regardless, the fact was that he hadn't come clean,

which had frustrated and tormented her, so she'd kept her peace and continued on with her plan to torment *him*.

She felt fairly sure she'd succeeded.

Maybe someday, when this fiasco had come to an end, they'd return to that very same dressing room and finish what they'd started. Quietly. Discreetly. She allowed the fantasy to play out a bit before a soft laugh emerged. Okay, they probably wouldn't do that—at least, not in a public dressing room—but the thought, and the image, was very, very nice.

Of course, she'd bought the nightgown. Soon, she hoped, she'd have the opportunity to model it for Cole again, this time without a game between them. On Christmas Eve, maybe. The outcome then would be far more fulfilling, for both of them.

Rachel moved to the other side of the room and opened the curtains, letting the midmorning sunshine roll in. After leaving the "store no man should ever have to set foot in"—as Cole had called the lingerie store—he'd suddenly become hell-bent on finishing the shopping for Mary as fast as possible. He had, in fact, dragged Rachel by the arm from one store to another.

She'd let him, somewhat amused by how the tempo of the game had changed. Before, he'd been all about taking it slow, henpecking every suggestion of Rachel's to death. But on Tuesday afternoon, he hadn't even hesitated. If she said to buy something, he bought it.

Even when she was being sarcastic. Such as the ridiculously large box of chocolates she'd pointed out as a joke, saying since "Mary" was his sweetheart, he could show her that by giving her enough sweets to last her a year. He'd nodded, grimly walked to the register, and a few minutes later had it in his possession.

From there on, Rachel purposely suggested gifts that

were on the cutesy, ludicrous or somewhat lame side—
at least so far as romantic gift choices were—just to see
what he'd do. He bought every one of them, without putting up any type of a fuss at all.

When they were done, Cole had purchased the red silk
negligee, the chocolates, a T-shirt that said "My Heart
Belongs to Him" with an arrow pointing to the right, a
stuffed toy poodle that yipped when you squeezed her—
Rachel couldn't resist that one—and finally, a package
of glow-in-the-dark, heart-shaped temporary tattoos.

The second the last gift was bought and bagged, Cole
had driven her to her car, hugged her tight and as she'd
let herself out, had mumbled something about "a cold
shower."

Yes, she'd absolutely succeeded in tormenting him,
which explained his frenzied need to finish shopping for
Mary. Delightful, really. Rachel wasn't done, though.
She wouldn't be done until Cole decided he'd had enough
and spilled the beans on what he'd been up to. Then…
well, then she couldn't wait to tell him all that was in
her heart.

Settling her hands on her hips, Rachel looked around
the bedroom. Everything was ready in here. She'd already dusted, vacuumed and folded the laundry. Other
than emptying the dishwasher, the kitchen was clean
and the refrigerator was stocked.

She had a few hours to kill before picking up her
mother at the airport. If Cole wasn't working, she'd
spend the time with him. Since he was, she did the next
best thing—she sat down at her desk, powered on her
computer and planned out her next move, with the beautiful vase Cole had given her in easy view. The vase,
regardless of the rest, would be her favorite gift this
Christmas. Maybe forever.

The stuffed toy poodle, however, came in at a very close second. Rachel chuckled as she searched online for local jewelry stores. Cupcake, indeed.

The Grinch had returned, grumpier and meaner and unhappier than ever. Cole paced in his kitchen, avidly ignoring the pile of gifts on his table. He'd brought them all out here to do what, he didn't know. He'd even wrapped them. Why?

Who was he giving them to now?

Nobody. That was who. He supposed he could return them, every last one, but he knew he wouldn't be able to. Stupid and inane, but those gifts—the first five of them—represented his hope and belief in a future that would now never come into being.

Returning them would be emotionally akin to tossing Rachel out of his life forever, and that was something he would never, in a million years, do. He wasn't capable of that.

Would *never* be capable of losing Rachel forever.

Friends, then. He was accustomed to playing that role in her life. He'd adjust again, once she returned to New York and they reverted to their normal text, email and sporadic phone call circle of communication. It was just now, while she was here, so soon after learning she was in love with another man, that made the prospect of mere friendship difficult to bear.

God, he'd lied to her today. Told her that he was working all day, when in fact, he wasn't going in until this evening. He'd told her the same yesterday, too. Well, that and he'd had a date with Mary yesterday evening. What a joke.

Tomorrow, though, he'd see Rachel. She'd asked, and

he couldn't cancel or make up more excuses, couldn't say anything but, "Yup. Sounds good, Rach." So he had.

Cole stopped pacing, went to his spare bedroom closet and found a box he'd filled with books. Without really thinking about what he was doing, he removed each and every book and stacked them on the floor. He'd figure out what to do with them later.

In the kitchen again, he carefully put the gifts he'd bought with Rachel in his head, in his heart, into the box and sealed it shut. Stared at it for all of ten seconds and cursed. Loudly.

He'd made a—what did teenage girls call them? Oh—a friggin' memory box. Lovely. Just lovely. Shaking his head, disgusted with himself, he carried the box to the spare room and tucked it back into the closet. Someday, maybe, he'd be able to get rid of them.

For now, though, he'd made his bed and he'd have to lie in it. And that meant keeping the charade going until Rachel was gone. Then, after a few weeks, he'd tell her his relationship with Mary had ended. No harm, no foul, right? Just as he'd planned if events turned out this way.

Too bad he hadn't really expected that to be the case.

Too bad that he'd been about as wrong as a man could get. Cole kicked the box, slammed the closet door shut and left the room. Harm had been done, all right. To him. But hell, he couldn't blame anyone but himself for that one, could he?

The best—the very best—he could do was ascertain this miserable outcome didn't affect Rachel's perspective toward their friendship. That would *have* to work. That would *have* to be good enough. Eventually, his focus would realign, his heart would heal and his perspective would match hers. And all of this would fade into the past.

* * *

She hadn't shown. Rachel had waited at the airport in the luggage claim area for a full hour before realizing that Candace Merriday had not made her flight.

Worry crept in, and then fear. Rachel's mother was not known for being uncommunicative, that was for sure. If she'd simply missed her flight, Rachel believed she would have phoned to tell her, probably with her new flight arrangements already set.

So yes, this was…odd. Atypical. And disturbing.

Knowing she wouldn't be able to hear a dang thing while in the airport, Rachel waited until she was in her car to call her mom. Candace answered immediately, thank goodness.

"Mom? What happened?" Rachel asked. "Is everything okay?"

"Everything is most definitely not okay," Candace said, her temper and frustration pouring through the line. "Your father is behaving like a…a jackass!"

"I see," Rachel said slowly, trying not to laugh. Laughing would be wrong. Her mother was obviously upset. But it was difficult, mainly because Candace Merriday rarely cursed, and when she did, never with such enthusiasm. "Is that why you're not here?"

"What? No, I—" She broke off, took a breath. "My goodness, today is Thursday. I…guess I forgot, what with the turmoil your father is putting me through!"

"You forgot the day or that you were coming here?" Rachel asked, shocked beyond belief. Mom's entire life was dictated by whatever was written in her appointment calendar.

"Both. Oh, darling, I'm so sorry. How thoughtless of me."

Normally, Rachel would agree. Not in this case. It was

just too…dammit, there was that word again, atypical. "It isn't like you to forget anything, Mom." Squeezing her eyes shut, she asked the one question she'd been attempting to avoid for days, "What's going on with Dad?"

She expected a flood of over-the-top emotion, a detailed explanation of every recent grievance—real or imagined—her father had put her mother through and then a sobbing plea to "talk some sense into your father, Rachel. He listens to you."

What she got was, "He's asked for a divorce, Rachel. I believe he's serious."

For years upon years, Rachel had waited to hear these words. Heck, during some of her parents' particularly rough spots, she'd *prayed* to hear them. Now that she had, she found the last thing she wanted to do was stand up and cheer.

"Tell me what happened, Mom," she said, attempting to mask the strange emotions *she* was experiencing. "Why does Dad want a divorce?"

And then she leaned back in her car, closed her eyes and listened.

Chapter Ten

The quote, "What a tangled web we weave, when we first practice to deceive," circled endlessly in Cole's head, like the lyrics of one of those blasted songs you couldn't get rid of, no matter how hard you tried. His fault, again, for many reasons. Not the least of which was underestimating Rachel's enthusiasm toward helping him woo his girlfriend.

Who'd have guessed she'd take to it so…passionately?

But this…well, he should have anticipated this. Even a lame-brained idiot knew that proper proposal protocol entailed a man on one knee with a certain piece of jewelry clutched tight in his sweaty hand. Yeah, Cole absolutely should have seen this one coming from a mile away. It was a sad, sad state of affairs that he hadn't.

Thirty minutes earlier, he'd met Rachel for coffee at the Beanery. His assumption had been that they'd chat, maybe go for a walk and she would hightail it back to Andrew. Wrong.

Oh, they'd had the coffee. Had gone for that walk. Along the way, she'd asked him about his proposal, about what he planned on saying to Mary. He'd flubbed that bit up good, muttering that he hadn't really given the actual proposal a lot of thought yet.

Rachel had given him what could only be described as a pitying look and dragged him here, to a jewelry store. To choose, of all things, an engagement ring for Mary.

Cole's father had warned him not to take his plan too far out of bounds. He was damn confident that Paul Foster would declare buying a diamond ring with no one to give it to as being too far out of bounds. But hell, what was he supposed to do about that now?

The manager, an older gentleman with a receding hairline, ushered Cole and Rachel to a glass counter on the far end of the room. "I've put together a lovely selection of rings, based on our phone call yesterday," he said to Rachel. "If these aren't right, we'll look at other options."

She'd phoned ahead? Cole mentally shook himself. Passionate? Try vehement. He had to find a way out of this.

"Thank you," she said somewhat absently. "I'm sure we'll find the perfect ring."

"Maybe I should do this on my own." Desperation clung to his voice. "The ring a man gives a woman should be special, something he chooses to reflect… um…their love and commitment and…it should be personal." He nodded, hoping he'd sounded convincing enough. "Yes. Better, I think, if I come back later. By myself."

"You're being silly again," she said. "We're here now,

so why not just take a look? If you don't find what you want, or need more time to consider, you can return later."

That was enough of an out for Cole. He'd look but wouldn't buy. Easy enough. Capitulating, he shrugged and said, "Sure. That's okay, I guess."

The sales manager beamed and unlocked the display case, saying, "Many a nervous young man comes through these doors, and I can assure you they do much better when they have help in making their selection."

"See, Cole? It's good that I'm with you." Rachel squeezed his hand, as if offering support. Other than her insistence in bringing him here, she'd been quieter than usual today, less sarcastic, too. Tired, maybe.

Possible reasons for her tiredness ticked off in his brain, each one causing his stomach to spasm with acid. Hell. If she'd modeled that nightgown for Andrew, then... *No*.

He was not allowing his thoughts to go there.

Winking, the manager brought out a long, narrow, black velvet display sheet that held one glittering diamond ring after another. "So," he said with another wink, "let's find the diamond that will make your lady swoon, shall we?"

The following forty-five minutes were a combination of odd and otherworldly. While not quite as uncomfortable as Cole had assumed, the discussion surrounding each ring—from the diamond's clarity and cut, to the setting, to the band itself—white gold versus yellow gold versus platinum versus titanium—left him feeling slightly on the nauseous side.

Fortunately, Rachel and the manager carried on that discussion just fine without him. All he had to do was hold the ring, turn it over in his fingers as if he were considering that specific ring's merits and listen. Every now and again, he'd toss in an "Ah," or a "Hmm," or an "Oh."

A method that seemed to be working quite well. Cole wasn't asked for his opinion, or told to take a second look when he'd pass the ring back to the store manager. Rachel didn't pester him with questions about what Mary would like or if he preferred one cut over another.

Everything was going along about as well as humanly possible, considering the ridiculous set of circumstances Cole was in, until…well, until the manager passed him *the* ring.

Rachel's ring.

And damn if he didn't hear the sound of trumpets blaring in his ears, feel the earth come to a grinding halt and came this-close to kneeling down and actually proposing. God help him, please. Somehow, and he didn't have a clue *how,* Cole reined in his nonsensical reaction and just stared at the ring. The perfect damn ring, right here, in his hands. The ring he would buy, regardless of its cost, if Rachel was his to propose to.

This time, he actually paid attention as the store manager and Rachel went into their discussion about the ring. He heard words such as, "art deco," "hexagonal frame," "hand engraved filigree crown," "platinum setting," "vintage," and "one-point-five carats."

Huh. None of that meant anything to him. Nor, as it turned out, did he care. His gut had identified the ring as being the right ring. That was all that mattered to Cole.

Rachel and the manager stopped talking and waited for Cole to make his general, not interested comment, and return the ring, like he had with every other one.

When he didn't, the other man chuckled. "This is the one, isn't it? I'd recognize that expression anywhere. A beautiful choice, young man. A spectacular ring that any woman would be pleased and proud to wear."

"Can I see it, Cole?" Rachel asked, her voice soft and hesitant and warm. "If that's okay with you, I mean. I wouldn't want to…" Her voice dropped off and she shrugged.

"Of course you can see the ring, Rach," he said, handing it over. He wasn't actually considering *buying* the darn thing, now was he? No. Of course not.

That would fall into the extreme end of impulse shopping.

She held the ring up for a closer view, twisting the band in her fingers as she did. A breathy sigh escaped and her blue eyes darkened to the same shade as the nightgown he'd about died seeing her in. That was one image he'd never forget.

This one, too, he thought, watching her as she was now, with her hair alight from the sunlight streaming in the store windows, her cheeks a rosy pink, her lips a touch more red, holding the ring for which he'd give away his last possession to see on her finger.

"Beautiful and spectacular," she said. "I…love it. I mean, you probably don't care what I think, but if you do…care, that is…I love it."

"Try the ring on," he said before he could think the request through. "I…I need to see how it looks on… er…a woman's hand."

Blink. Blink. Pause and blink. "Oh, no. That wouldn't be right. Not at all." She shook her head back and forth. "No one should put on an engagement ring before the proposal. Bad luck."

"I don't believe in luck. Good or bad." He composed his features, unwilling to show exactly how much he wanted to see Rachel wearing the ring he would choose for her. "Friends, remember? I helped you out at the… mall. Help me out now. Please?"

"I really, really don't want to."

"Come on, Rach," he said, going for nonchalance. "What's the big deal?"

"It's a huge deal," she whispered, looking from the ring to him. "I… Are you sure, Cole? Are you really, really sure you want me to put on this ring, right now?"

"I'm really, really, *really* sure."

"Fine." Confusion and uncertainty colored her expression. "If…if that's what you want."

Her hand—hell, her entire body—visibly trembled as she brought the ring to her right hand, as she started to slip the band on her right ring finger.

Reaching over, he stopped her, took the ring and grasped her left hand. "Wrong hand, Rach," he said. He swallowed, hard, and slid the ring—Rachel's ring—on her finger.

And hell if he didn't tremble a bit himself.

There. Glorious. Perfect. The way it *should* be. Every image he'd ever had of them, the past that had actually occurred and the future he'd hoped for, flashed like a movie reel behind his eyes. He loved this woman. He would probably always love this woman.

But she wasn't meant for him.

All of his prior concerns seemed silly. Meaningless. Oh, he knew they weren't. Not really. If Rachel loved him like he loved her, they would have had no choice but to clear the air in order to build a steady, longstanding foundation for their future.

In this minute, though, in this tiny speck of time, all Cole saw was a myriad of lost opportunities. Why the hell hadn't he said something before? Why had he focused so much on the past, instead of taking control of the future? Stupid. Such a stupid waste.

"I won't be buying a ring today," he said to the store manager. Then, once Rachel had removed the ring and pushed it across the counter, he took her by the hand and led her outside.

"What's wrong, Cole?" she asked. She always could read him rather well.

"We need to talk," he said quietly. He couldn't end the entire charade, but he damn well could put part of it to rest. "I've changed my mind. I won't be proposing to…Mary."

Every drop of color drained from Rachel's skin. She blinked a few times, lifted her chin and swept her gaze somewhere off to his left. "All right," she said in a smooth, emotionless, almost robotic voice. "Let's talk. Where to?"

"How does my place sound?" he asked. He was about to lie through his teeth. Some privacy was in order, and her place wouldn't work. Not with Andrew in residence.

She redirected her focus to him, nodded. "That's fine," she said in that same odd tempo. "I'll drive myself and meet you there."

Nervous butterflies flipped and flew in Rachel's stomach as she waited for Cole to join her in his living room. Currently, he was in the kitchen, making them coffee. She didn't really want any, didn't need the caffeine screwing with her already freaked-out system, but holding the mug would give her something to do with her hands.

She breathed in through her nose, out through her mouth, fidgeted on the couch and tried to calm her racing heart. Had she screwed up in taking Cole to the jewelry store? Maybe.

Her sole objective in teasing him and tormenting him with engagement rings was to push him into admitting the truth, so he'd drop the Mary pretense once and for all. Instead, he'd insisted she try on a ring—a beautiful, to-die-for, every-woman's-fantasy type of ring.

The thought of doing so had crippled her.

When he'd grabbed her left hand to slip the ring on her himself, her legs had weakened and goose bumps had sheathed her skin. One look at Cole, at the determination gleaming in his eyes and the hard set of his jaw, had told her this was about to be a very important moment.

And it had been. Oh, yes. Just not in the way she'd thought.

He hadn't come clean. He hadn't professed his love. And no, he sure as heck hadn't proposed. Rachel shivered and rubbed her arms briskly. She hadn't thought—not even for a second—that he was about to propose in the middle of the jewelry store, before they'd even told each other their feelings, so the fact he hadn't was fine.

What wasn't, what had chilled her and petrified her in equal measures, were the words "I've changed my mind," followed by "We need to talk."

She crossed her legs. Uncrossed them. And then crossed them again.

It wasn't as if she hadn't already had plenty of adrenaline and anxiety to deal with after yesterday and this morning's repeated and nonstop phone calls from her parents.

No, her father had not asked for a divorce. He had hinted at one, however. Rachel knew this because she'd called dear-old-Dad as soon as she'd hung up with her mom.

The details were pretty clear, actually. Dad, finally tired of waging war with his wife, had suggested marriage counseling. Mom said no, she didn't want to air their "dirty laundry" in front of a stranger. That was when Rachel's father had hinted at a divorce.

Of course, none of that explained their penchant for drawing Rachel into their issues. Or, she supposed, her inability to remove herself from those issues, despite her many attempts.

They hadn't yet asked her to return home to "mediate," but they would. Sooner or later. She sighed, fidgeted again. Concern for both of her parents pooled inside, mixing with all of her other unsettled emotions. Even so, she wouldn't go home to mediate. Not this time.

But she couldn't ignore what was happening, either.

Cole walked into the room, carrying two large mugs filled with steaming coffee. He set hers on the end table closest to her and then moved to the chair catty-corner to the sofa.

Neither spoke for a good thirty seconds, though it felt more like an eternity. Resisting the urge to squirm, Rachel picked up her coffee and took a small sip. Good and strong and sweet.

"Asking for your help was wrong," Cole said, breaking the silence, his voice heavy and deliberate. And, Rachel noted, very, very sure. "So...I'm sorry for doing that. I shouldn't have dragged you into my...romantic dilemma."

"You don't need to apologize for asking a friend for help," Rachel said. She gripped her cup tighter, striving for balance. "At the jewelry store, you said you'd changed your mind. I thought you wanted to talk about that. Is... is this about something else?"

Please, please say yes, Rachel thought, *tell me this*

*is about your feelings, about us, about something real.
Please.*

Oh, God. Please.

"I was so sure, you see. So damn sure of my feel-ings, that I barged ahead without thinking a damn thing through." He stood, started pacing the length of the living room. "And then I saw that ring on your finger, and everything inside went cold."

"Just that fast, huh?" Rachel closed her eyes, breathed and reminded herself of one very fortunate fact: Cole did not know that she knew. If she kept her voice calm, her behavior as normal as possible, he would never know that she knew. "You must have had doubts before, or simply seeing a ring on a woman's finger wouldn't have done that to you."

"What relationship doesn't include doubts?" He stopped pacing, placed his palms against the wall and leaned his body forward. "I had doubts, have for a while," he admitted. "But I stupidly thought I could overlook all of them."

"Does this…um…have to do with the serious con-cerns you brought up last week?" The concerns they'd never discussed. "About…Mary?"

His body stilled. "Yup. I…realized today, when you had that damn ring on your finger, that I'd taken this too far. Everything suddenly seemed serious and…real, I guess. Too real, with the problems between me and Mary."

Dammit! She wanted him to stop speaking in code. Wanted him to say straight-out what he was thinking, and *who* he was thinking those things about.

She pulled together every last bit of courage she'd ever had in her entire life, sat up straight and said, "Why don't we play a game of pretend, Cole? Just for a few minutes. It might help clear a few things up. Maybe...I can still help you with your romantic dilemma."

He lowered his forehead until it touched the wall. "Go on. What type of game?"

"You and I have a troubled history. One in which we've never properly discussed." Oh, dear Lord, was she really doing this? Yes. She was. "So if we pretend—just for a few minutes, mind you—that *I* am Mary, maybe we can talk through this using our experiences."

Pushing himself off of the wall, he faced her. Ran one hand over his jaw. "Is that a good idea, Rachel? There are a lot of words between us we've never said about that time in our lives."

She went to take a sip of her coffee, noticed how badly her hands were shaking and carefully set the cup down. "Maybe it's time we did, then. Maybe, in addition to helping you with your concerns regarding Mary, it will help us, as well. Our friendship."

"Our friendship has survived in spite of our never getting into any of this."

Hurt was there. She saw it, glittering in his dark, dark eyes. Hurt *she* had put there.

"Maybe so," she admitted, her heart heavier than ever before. "But surviving isn't the same as flourishing." Afraid she'd back away—*run* away—if she didn't dive in, she pulled in a breath and...dived. "I know I hurt us, Cole. I know I hurt *you*. I'm the one who's sorry."

Anger replaced the hurt, but it glittered just as brightly. "Four years, Rachel."

"I know."

"Four years since you left my hospital room, promising to return as soon as possible."

"I know," she repeated. "Cole—"

"You *never* returned," he said. "Not until I invited you."

"You're right. I didn't." She shoved her hands under her thighs. "When I left, I was confused and scared. My father called, but you know that, and with the way things were with you, with us, it seemed—and I'm so ashamed to admit this—easier to leave."

He shook his head as if he had water in his ear. "Explain."

So she did, slowly and calmly, enunciating every word and doing her utmost best to keep her emotions from leaking through. She told him how she hadn't known who to be with him—his friend or his girlfriend—how lost she'd felt, and how because of that, going to her parents had held an odd sense of comfort.

All of which had to have sounded incredibly lame and weak considering the struggles Cole had faced at the time. But her words, every one of them, were the honest to God truth. Whether he understood them or not, accepted them or not, hated her forever or…loved her, she wouldn't embellish on why she'd done what she'd done.

To do so would be unfair and…as wrong as leaving in the first place.

One tear, and then another, dripped down Rachel's cheeks. Irritated with herself, she wiped them away. She didn't want Cole to think she was after his sympathy, or an easy path to forgiveness. Her emotions were just too raw, too…fragile to hold in.

"I'm sorry," she mumbled, still wiping her tears. "I'm so sorry for abandoning you when you needed me, for not being the friend you deserved. I really let you down. I'll…I'll never forgive myself for that. Never in a million-and-one years."

He closed his eyes, let out a long sigh. "You're being too hard on yourself."

"Oh, no. That is one thing I'm not doing."

A heavy, weighted silence hung between them. Finally, Cole opened his eyes again, shoved his thumbs in his jean pockets. "Tell me why you didn't come back until last year."

His gaze was steady and sure, waiting.

"You told me not to," she said simply, even though the memory hurt. "I didn't feel as if I would be welcome until I knew you were ready to see me. That you *wanted* to see me."

That also was the truth.

Cole's brow furrowed. "I was hurt, Rachel. In every way a man can be hurt. I shouldn't have said that, but *you* should have tried again. The next day. The next week. The next month. You shouldn't have given up. *I* wouldn't have given up."

"I know that! God, don't you think I know that about you? I know who you are, Cole."

She went to him then, her tears running faster and harder, her heart exploding with pain and loss and sorrow, and reached for him...so she could hug him or kiss him or what, exactly, she didn't know. All she knew was that she had to touch him, comfort him. Be there for him.

If he would let her.

Cole took a jerky step backward and looked at her as if she had lost her mind.

"I'm sorry," she repeated, stunned and hurt and shamed all over again. "You don't know how sorry I am, how much I wish I could turn back the clock and change our past. Change *my* behavior. I would, Cole. Know that, please, if nothing else."

He swallowed and nodded. Combed his fingers

through his hair. Looked at her long and hard, all the way to her soul, and deeper yet.

"I do know that," he said finally. "I know who you are too, Rachel. I really, really do."

Relief unfurled inside, swift and all-encompassing. Trusting her instincts, believing he wouldn't reject her again, she went to him. He accepted her, pulled her tight to his chest, stroked her hair and soothed her tears. A sense of security, of rightness, overcame her.

This was home. It was as simple and complicated as that.

"Do you think we'll be able to move past this?" she whispered into his shoulder. For a devastating few minutes there, she'd been sure she was going to lose him entirely. She never wanted to feel that way again. "Can you forgive me?"

There wasn't even a heartbeat of a pause. "I've already forgiven you, sweetheart."

"Okay, that's…that's good. I'm… Thank you."

"Welcome. Thing is, Rach, this isn't all on your shoulders." He pulled back and tipped her chin up with his fingers, so they were eye to eye. "I had my own demons to contend with, and I should've said something about this before now. Can you forgive me?"

"Yes," she said. And it really was that easy. "Of course I can."

"Whew," he said, miming wiping sweat from his forehead. "Glad our friendship is solid."

Wait a minute. He'd just said he'd forgiven her, had said they'd be able to move past this, had even asked her to forgive him. Rachel stepped back, needing the space to think.

"Did…um…this help you at all with your Mary dilemma?" She slid her palms down her jeans, waited and

hoped and prayed a little, too. "I mean, if you can forgive me—"

"Mary and I are over," Cole said abruptly, with a fi-
nality no one would question. "What I can forgive my
friends for is a fair bit different than what I can forgive
my potential wife for. I made a mistake thinking otherwise. A mistake I'll correct as soon as I...as soon as
I can."

"Oh," Rachel whispered, fighting back a new on-
slaught of tears. Uh-uh. No more crying. Not here, not
when she wouldn't explain the reason why to the man
who had just broken her heart. And he didn't have a
clue in his thick skull. Not. A. One. "That's...too bad."

"Don't look so sad, Rach. Mary will be fine. Hell,
I doubt she'll even miss me." Cole gave her his wide,
charming grin, and came close enough to chuck her chin.
As if she were his sister. "You and I are good, though.
Forever friends, right?"

Well, seeing as that was the best they were ever going
to be, she'd take it. Of course she would. But she would
never stop longing for what they didn't have, what they
couldn't have.

"Yes," she said softly, quietly. "Forever friends. Just
like always."

There was a dim light visible at the end of the dark
tunnel. Cole would never know how close she had come
to spilling her heart, to telling him how much she loved
him.

Pride, it seemed, worked fairly well as a silver lining.

Chapter Eleven

A night of sleepless tossing and turning had made one point abundantly clear to Rachel. She couldn't spend this Christmas in Steamboat Springs, Colorado. After last night's episode with Cole, she needed to put some distance between them.

But not forever and most definitely not like before. Never like before.

However, right now she needed to be somewhere that Cole wasn't, just for a little while. Some place where every last thing didn't remind her of him. Somewhere she could lick her wounds, find a sense of stability again and come to terms with all that had occurred. And she needed to do these things in a place she wouldn't—couldn't—accidently bump into Cole.

He knew her too well. Even when they were kids she was never able to hide her misery from him for very long. He'd poke, prod and badger relentlessly, asking questions until she broke down and shared every last detail. It would be no different this time. And how in the world would their friendship recover from that? She truly didn't think it would.

Added in to all of those very valid reasons, her parents needed her. They had called, as she'd known they would. And yes, they'd each asked her to return to New York, just as she'd also known they would. Each blaming the other. Each saying that Rachel's presence was needed for the other. And yes, she'd agreed. Of course she had.

Because she couldn't stay here. Because they needed her. Both valid reasons.

This time, though, she would not become their private tennis ball. Oh, she would be there for them to offer comfort and her support. Just being there was important, as well. Especially with a word such as *divorce* being bandied about.

She still didn't know how she felt about that possibility. Not really. At the end of it all, whether her parents stayed married or not, she wanted them to find some peace. Hell. All of them, including Rachel, needed to find some peace.

So, yes, she'd be there for them. They were her family, after all. But she wouldn't fall into the accustomed routine. She might still be their daughter, but she wasn't a child any longer, she was an adult. As an adult, she'd sit down with them individually, explain her limits and go from there. One day at a time, one issue at a time. Maybe, if she held her ground, they'd eventually meet her halfway. Well, with any luck at all, she hoped they would.

If they didn't, she'd cross that bridge when she came to it.

Rachel pulled her suitcase from the closet and began

the process of packing for her return trip. She'd been lucky to find a flight the weekend before Christmas. Luckier yet to find a flight that left this evening. She'd be home by ten and tucked into her own bed by eleven. Then, tomorrow she'd wake up in New York and would begin the process of healing.

The second she regained her equilibrium, Rachel would make plans to return for a normal, non-crazy visit with Cole. And this time, she wouldn't wait for an invitation.

When she'd finished with her suitcase, she turned her attention toward the Christmas tree. It hadn't even been up a full week, and already it had to come down. It was sad, but not the saddest element in her life at the moment, so she went to work removing the ornaments one at a time. She wrapped and placed each one back in its box, fighting off the memories they held. There was no time to linger, no time to dwell on what each lovely ball of glass meant.

Rachel closed the lid on the ornament box and started untwisting the lights. When the tree was achingly bare, she hauled it to the curb, where it looked—in her current state of mind—sad and forlorn and...well, rejected.

She continued on this way, handling each necessary task with a businesslike attitude, mentally checking off items from her to-do list as she went. Throughout it all, she stifled her emotions, working to keep them even and her mind blank, and just kept pushing forward. If it were at all possible, she'd rather not shed one more tear until she was safely in another state.

Finally, she exhaled a shaky breath and walked around the house, one room at a time, ascertaining she hadn't forgotten anything that she wanted to take back with her to New York. The list was small. A few books she hadn't gotten to, her cell-phone charger and—when she returned to her bedroom—the vase Cole had given her. That stupid vase.

That stupid, beloved, beautiful vase burst her moratorium on tears into smithereens. Dammit, she didn't want to cry. Didn't want to sink into that black hole of misery again. Didn't want to be reminded of the very many ways she'd screwed up.

She sucked in a gulping breath, and then another, and tried to calm down. But the tears kept falling. Her throat closed, her chest balled up so tight it hurt and her sobs became an unrelenting, powerful explosion that she couldn't begin to stop.

"This sucks!" she yelled into the empty room. "Sucks, sucks, sucks!"

Stomping over to the vase, she picked it up and stared at it, ran her finger along the row of tiny, hand-painted flowers Cole had said reminded him of her eyes, and then, because she could conceive of no other action to take, crawled into her bed.

She curled up beneath the quilt, dragging it over her head, shutting out the world and embraced the pain. Pressing the vase to her chest, she gave in to the overwhelming grief assaulting her and allowed herself a good old-fashioned cry.

When she had no more tears left to shed, she gasped raggedly one last time before crawling out from beneath her tomb. Dry, hollow and hurting down to her toes, she gently set the vase on her desk and very purposefully grabbed her suitcase.

She wouldn't take the vase home with her, it would be too painful, would stir up too many emotions, too many memories. Rachel firmly closed the bedroom door, shutting the pain inside. She wouldn't come upstairs again during this visit.

Four hours until she had to leave for the airport. Everything she'd had to do here was done, the house was prepared to sit empty for…who knew how long? Rachel closed her eyes and squeezed her hands into tight fists, counted to ten and straightened her spine.

There was only one item left on her to-do list. An essential item. One task yet to complete. And one that would very likely have her crying all the way to the airport.

The only thing she had to do now was say goodbye to Cole.

For the entire day, Cole had gone over the prior night's events with a fine-tooth comb, rehashing every word, every look, every flicker of Rachel's eyelashes.

What was it? What had he missed?

He kept thinking there was something there, something that hadn't seemed important at the time, some bit of information that he hadn't latched on to, but damn if he could locate it. All he had was this…buzzing in his brain, this incessant push to keep at it, to nail down the mysterious something, and not to stop until he had identified it and figured out what it meant.

Problem was, he didn't know what he was looking for.

Cole finished ringing up his current customer and tried to set the insistent itching aside. Yesterday, in every way except for one, had been about as bad as a day could get. Still, having that talk with Rachel had been cathartic and necessary, for both of them. In the end, forgiving her was as easy as breathing. In the end, he'd realized he'd already forgiven her. He'd just needed to hear her explain, in her words, the whats and whys of the situation.

Forgiving himself, though…well, that was another story altogether.

If he'd just broached his concerns earlier, they might have had a chance. If she'd explained her side of things earlier, they still might have had a chance. Basically, from Cole's point of view, they'd both behaved foolishly. They were, from an outside perspective, equally to blame. Why, then, did he feel as if the burden of guilt rested solely on his shoulders?

The bell on the door rang, announcing a customer's entrance. Cole glanced up with a welcoming smile, ready to ask if he could be of any help. His smile widened. Instead of some random person, his gaze landed on Rachel. As always, the sight of her warmed him from the inside out, made him feel more alive. She just had that affect on him. Even now.

Approaching the counter, she whisked her hair over one ear. He noticed right off that she looked a tad on the pale side, as if she hadn't slept well. That bothered him.

"You're a sight for sore eyes, darlin'," he said with an easy grin. "I was just thinking I could use a coffee break. Feel like walking over to the Beanery?"

Haley was supposed to leave in a few, but Cole figured he could sweet talk his sister into staying for thirty extra minutes. Besides which, the only surefire way he knew of to realign his focus, to put Rachel solidly in the friend category, was to spend time with her.

Normal time. Doing stuff friends did. Like grabbing a coffee together.

"I'm sorry, Cole, I can't," she said softly, hesitantly, in the same odd beat she'd had yesterday. "That's actually what I stopped by to tell you."

"You stopped by to tell me you can't go to the Beanery? Impressive, Rach, seeing how I just now asked."

Okay, it was a lame joke, but Cole had recognized the precursor to bad news.

He was, he found, exhausted to the bone from hearing bad news.

"No, no. That wasn't what I meant." She scraped her teeth over her bottom lip, darted her gaze downward. "I came to tell you that…well, that I'm leaving. Tonight."

"You're leaving?" he asked, feeling like an imbecile for doing the statement-to-question thing he teased her for, but he needed clarification. Urgently. "As in leaving Steamboat Springs, tonight, with Christmas a mere three days away?"

"Yes," she said in more of a sigh than anything else. Her eyes, he noted, had a hollow quality that also bothered him. "I made the arrangements this morning."

"This morning?" He set aside his concerns as an old hurt rolled in. "And you're just telling me now?" Why did this feel like the other time she'd left, when the two instances bore little-to-no similarities?

For one thing, he wasn't lying injured in a hospital bed. And there weren't any doctors around, giving him dire warnings that his career was probably over. Finally, to his chagrin, even though he'd had the opportunity, he hadn't kissed Rachel less than twenty-four hours ago.

See? Not alike. In any friggin' way whatsoever.

"I was going to call, but that felt too impersonal." Her voice shook, a little, on that part. "Especially considering our conversation last night. So…I waited until I could come here, to see you and tell you in person. That was important to me, Cole."

Buzz, buzz, buzz went his brain again. What in blazes were his instincts trying to tell him?

"Why are you leaving?" he asked, hoping her answer

would give him a clue. "Did something happen that has upset you? Or…?"

"I'm fine." She blinked twice. Paused. Then blinked three times. "It's my parents."

Ah. Well, that required zero explanation. Now, he understood the shaky voice, the hollow eyes and her tiredness. "Sweetheart, you have to stop letting them do this to you. Why don't you stay here, as you originally planned?"

"I…can't. This time is different," she said stubbornly. "I have to go. They need me and I…well, I need to be there. In New York. With them. So…please try to understand."

His heart cracked in two.

"I do understand. You love your parents. Enough said." True, that. What he didn't comprehend was why two people had stayed together for so long when they continued to make each other, and their daughter, miserable. Rounding the counter, he opened his arms, needing to hold her one more time until the next time. Whenever that time was. "Come here, then, darlin'."

Emotion filled her eyes for a split second, so fast that Cole almost missed it. She was hurting, probably thinking of her parents and all they were going through. He had to admit that he wished he'd listened to Haley and had kidnapped Rachel days ago.

It would have solved everything. She'd be safe with him. He'd see to that. And his heart wouldn't feel as if someone had beaten it with a sledgehammer.

In another second, Rachel filled his arms. She was soft and warm and smelled like she always did, and Cole never wanted to let her go. So, he did the next best thing, the only thing he could do in this particular space of time, minutes before she walked out of his life again. He held her close to him and cherished the moment, fleeting as it was, with every beat of his heart.

When they separated, Cole cradled her face with his hands and looked deep into her eyes, bent forward and kissed her lightly on the cheek. "Take care of yourself, Rachel. Promise me."

"I will. You do the same."

Emotion clogged his throat. Words seemed impossible. He nodded in reply, then walked her to the door and stood there, watching, until he couldn't see her any longer. Hell. Just…hell.

He ached, missing her already. Missed Rachel in the same desperate way Cole assumed he'd miss one of his limbs, or his hearing, or his eyesight. It was an intrinsic loss, deep and painful and unrelenting. Swearing under his breath, he stepped away from the door.

And a bolt of lightning hit him square between the shoulder blades. Metaphorically speaking, of course. There was something else he'd missed…not in an emotional sense, but in the physical. Andrew. Where the hell was Andrew? He hadn't come inside with Rachel, and he hadn't been in the car waiting for her… Cole had seen Rachel drive away, in a car, by herself.

So where was the man she professed to love? Cole couldn't believe Andrew would stay at the house here in Steamboat Springs if Rachel was headed back to New York. No, the man wouldn't do that. Staying here wouldn't be sensible, and from what Cole had seen and heard, Andrew was a very sensible man.

That meant…Andrew was not in Steamboat Springs. He'd already returned to New York. But when had he returned? Earlier today, yesterday, last week?

The buzzing in Cole's brain got louder, stronger, even

more insistent. Andrew wasn't with Rachel. Andrew wasn't with Rachel. Oh, hell.

Andrew wasn't with Rachel.

Chapter Twelve

After putting the car in gear, Rachel eased onto the road. Emotion roiled in her stomach, sending waves of nausea through her body. Tightening her trembling fingers around the steering wheel, she mentally straightened her spine and forced herself not to turn the car around.

Not to run back to Cole with her heart in her hands.

God, she wanted to. The idea compelled her, pulled at her, pleaded with her to take a freaking chance. But... she just couldn't. Too scary, for one thing. Way too damn scary.

And for another, this trip home was necessary. Her parents really did need her.

Besides which, what good would staying in Steamboat Springs serve, anyway? Nothing would change with Cole. He'd made that perfectly clear last night, when he'd said, "What I can forgive my friends for is a fair bit different than what I can forgive my potential wife for. I made a mistake thinking otherwise."

Those words, the tenor and cadence of his voice, the firm set of his jaw and the determination all but gleaming in his eyes, refused to leave her brain. Or her heart.

So, no. Staying wouldn't serve to make anything better, or easier. It would only make her feel worse—more wounded, more sad, more lonely, more everything than she already felt right now. Easier—so much easier—to flee from here, from Cole, and rebuild her strength before returning, before once again embarking on another game of pretend: that she only thought of Cole as her friend. Her freaking forever friend.

"Friendship isn't so bad," she whispered to herself. "He's an amazing friend."

And he was. Somehow, though, his friendship—having only his friendship—no matter how amazing, seemed akin to one of those consolation prizes you won in a contest.

She yearned for the blue ribbon.

The twinkling Christmas lights lining the street blurred beneath another unwanted layer of pouring tears. Today, all she seemed to do was cry. She angrily wiped the wetness from her cheeks and tried to regain her earlier businesslike attitude. She couldn't. Not when she felt as if she had lost…everything that meant anything.

Dammit all! She'd so wanted to spend Christmas here, in Steamboat Springs, with Cole. She'd spent a childhood of Christmases here, after all. With him. Those Christmases she wasn't here had never felt right or complete. Hadn't even seemed real.

Okay, she was going home. To New York, where her parents waited. Where she was needed. Except…well, New York wasn't her home. This—Steamboat Springs—

was her home. Hadn't she always known that, in some form or fashion?

And then somehow, out of nowhere, the stupid vase Cole had given her whipped into her mind, and the image of it sitting on her desk brought about another rush of tears. Why had she left it there? She... No. She had to have the vase with her. She couldn't leave the gift Cole had bought her here, when she was in New York.

How could she live without seeing it, holding it, every day? Without having the physical reminder of his words, of how the color of the flowers had reminded him—

Out of nowhere, a feeling of peace enveloped Rachel. It wasn't the vase she couldn't live without—it was Cole. Love flowed through her as she thought about Cole's hug, the warmth and security of being in his arms, the way he'd looked at her when he held her face in his hands.

Cole was her home. And he lived here, so yes, that was why Steamboat Springs had always felt more her home than anywhere else she'd ever lived, had ever traveled to.

Rachel breathed in deeply. Okay, what was she going to do with these revelations? She needed a minute to think, to... She pulled into the first gas station she came to and threw the car into Park. Closing her eyes, she rested her forehead atop the steering wheel and took in another deep breath. She couldn't live without Cole.

The silly, silly man who'd created a girlfriend in order to romance her and had never come clean with her. He'd had more than enough chances to admit his lie, but he hadn't. Not even after she'd finally found the courage to discuss their past, her reasons for leaving...her mistake in not returning. Of course, he...

Well, he likely thought she loved Andrew. She hadn't

told him the truth about that, or that she'd figured out his game. Was she any better?

Oh, Lord. She had to go back. She had to give him— them—one more chance. How could she not? If she didn't, would she one day find herself in the same type of relationship as her parents? How close had she come to that with Andrew?

The thought was startling.

Rachel squared her shoulders. For once, her parents would have to wait. She'd always made them her top priority, running when they called, listening to their venting, bending to their requests. All the while, she'd never been able to help them. Not really.

Because they had to help themselves. That was their job, not hers.

Dropping the car into Drive, knowing she really had no other choice—not if she didn't want to spend the next four years mired in regret—she pulled back onto the road, heading in the opposite direction. Toward home.

Toward Cole.

And, she hoped, toward a future worth risking everything for.

Cole strode to the office, where Haley was gathering her belongings to leave. "Sorry, kid, but I'm going to need you to stay and close tonight. Don't argue, just nod and say yes."

Nodding, Haley said, "Yes. But…why?"

"Rachel's on her way to the airport, set on returning to New York," he said quickly, knowing his sister would understand his urgency. He pulled on his coat and shoved his hands in his pockets, searching for his keys. "I have to stop her before she gets on her plane."

"Oh!" His sister squealed. "This is so romantic. It's

like one of those movies where the guy chases the girl to the airport, but he gets there just as the plane is taking off. He's sad because he missed his great opportunity to tell her—" Haley stopped. Stared at Cole and wrinkled her nose. "Wait a minute. Why is she leaving so soon?"

"Long story." Dammit all. Where had he put his keys?

"Did you do something to upset her?"

His gaze swung around the room. "Have you seen my keys?"

"Nope, can't say that I have." She gave him a quizzical look, complete with squinty eyes and puckered lips. "Seriously, what did you do to her?"

"Nothing! I…I'm not quite sure what's happening, but something is." He shook his head, frustrated and anxious. "Help me find my keys. Or give me yours. Please."

Haley glanced over his shoulder, and her mouth split into a wide grin. "I don't think that will be necessary."

"Of course it's necessary. I need keys to drive. I need to drive to get to the airport. If I don't—" He stopped. Breathed. And listened to his senses.

Rachel. She was here. Right behind him. He knew that without question, without any hesitation. The buzzing in his brain subsided, his muscles relaxed and he inhaled a long, cleansing breath of relief. Everything might just be okay, after all.

"Welcome back, sweetheart," he said without turning around.

"It was the vase," Rachel said to Cole's back in thick, halting syllables. "That silly little squat vase you had to go and buy for me. That's why I'm here."

Facing her now, Cole nodded as if her words made perfect sense. They didn't. He couldn't care less what had brought her back. The fact was that she was here, right now, with him. And that meant he hadn't lost his chance.

Still, he went with it, saying, "I like the vase, Rach. I thought of you the second I saw it."

"Yes," she said in a whisper, looking far too serious and confused for his liking. "You…ah…mentioned that. But I'm here for… We need to—"

"Did I mention how the color of the flowers—the ones painted along the bottom—are the exact same shade of blue as your eyes?"

Her chin dipped in a slow, jerky nod, but a curious glint entered her gaze. Better. "Yes. You mentioned that, as well."

"Good. I thought I had," he said, slowing his cadence to a drawl. "I should also mention that your eyes tend to change colors based on your emotions."

One eyebrow arched. "You should mention that, huh?" she asked, no longer sounding weak or hesitant. In fact, she sounded downright spunky. Better yet. "Now?"

"Hmm. Yes." Cole took a step toward her. Stared into the eyes he loved so much. "See, right now, I wouldn't be able to say the color is an exact match to those flowers. Right now, your eyes are a good bit darker than normal. So, Rach, I have to ask—" he rubbed the pad of his thumb over the soft, fragile area beneath her eyes "—what are you feeling at this very second?"

Blink, blink, blink. "Really, Cole? That's what you want to know?"

"I do," he said matter-of-factly. "And that's a fact."

Suddenly, those eyes darkened another shade. "I see. A fact, huh? You know a lot about facts, don't you? Meaning, you have no issues determining fact from fiction, correct?"

"Fiction as in novels, darlin'?"

"Fiction as in games of pretend," she shot back. "Such as, oh…I don't know…make-believe friends. Or, in your case, girlfriends? Or at least, girl*friend*? Are you familiar with that concept, Cole?"

Her words shocked him. She knew? Well, hell. "Um."

She tapped her foot. "Um?"

Probably, he should beg for forgiveness. Later, he probably would. Right now, though, he decided to play this moment out for all of its worth. "Well, pretend girlfriends have a lot going for them, Rach. They don't chatter incessantly, or expect you to give up your night out with the guys." He ran his hand over his jaw, grinned. "Yeah. Fact is, I can see lots of reasons why a man might think a pretend girlfriend is better than a real one."

Her chin lifted an inch. "You, Cole Foster, are an idiot. Why—"

"Right, I am. A man in love often behaves idiotically," he said, grinning wider when her jaw snapped shut.

She regained her bearing fast. "Only an idiot, whether he's in love or not, would think creating a pretend girlfriend is the way to…romance another woman. Because yeah, that is so much better than being open and honest and—oh, I don't know—communicating!"

"You're absolutely right. Communicating would have been the better choice. But I'm curious, darlin'. How long have you known? Because I don't recall any discussion of that sort."

He winked. Waited. His mind replayed the last several days. She'd known for a while, he'd bet money on it. And she'd used that knowledge to turn his game on him.

It was, he decided, rather humorous.

Though she didn't appear amused. Tapping her foot harder, she glowered. "How long have I known that I'm Mary, otherwise known as Cupcake—which is, by the way, a ludicrous name to call a woman, even a pretend woman—and that you've been messing with my head—not to mention my heart—ever since I arrived in Steamboat Springs?" Retreating a step, she angled her arms over her chest. "Is that what you mean?"

Nope, not amused. This was not the same woman who'd walked in here. Well, she was here, and he'd take her—any which way or the other—but this woman was really annoyed with him. And hell, he couldn't blame her. He'd started the fiasco.

It was such an old cliché, but she was beautiful when she was angry. And frankly, while he'd prefer her happy, her shooting nails—even if they were aimed at his head—was better than confused. "Yes, darlin', that's exactly what I mean."

"Why, you—" Pausing, she bit her bottom lip. "What if I told you that I discovered this little fact the day after Andrew and I went our separate ways and he returned to New York?"

"I already figured out that Andrew left," he said lightly. In truth, he was as happy as all get-out to hear confirmation. "I just don't know when he left. Mind filling in the blank spots for me?"

She looked at him, blinked—he was really going to have to ask her if she needed glasses—and darn if her lips didn't twitch, just a little. Okay, anger was giving way to...well, he didn't know what, but he had a feeling they were headed down a path he wanted to be on.

Had waited for years to be on.

"Hmm. Let me see," she said, her voice just this side of husky. "It might have been...no, it wasn't that day." She paused, her lips twitched a bit more. "No wait, gee, it wasn't that day, either. Gosh, Cole," she said in an oh-so-innocent manner, "I simply just don't remember."

"Tell me when Andrew left, and I'll…give you a present," he cajoled with a teasing grin. Why he cared so much, he didn't know. But he had to know. "I have ten of them at home with your name on it."

She arched a brow. "My name or Mary's name? Or did you use 'Cupcake'?"

"Your name." Cole put his hand on his heart. "Honest. Only yours."

Those words softened her mouth and brought a glimmer of satisfaction to her smile. "Andrew left last Sunday morning. We… I realized he wasn't the man for me on Saturday. Realized, also, that I'd known that for quite a while."

A week. The man hadn't been in the picture at all for nearly a full week. The realization was both exhilarating and excruciating. Particularly when Cole imagined what might have happened in the dressing room if he'd known she'd chosen that gown with him in mind.

Him. Not Andrew.

And that meant, "So, you figured out what I was up to the day we went snow-tubing?"

"Um. I began to suspect." She darted a glance toward Haley. "I didn't really know until the next day, and that's when I planned my revenge. I'll admit I had a lot of fun with that."

Haley cleared her throat. "This is all so…weirdly sweet and cute, but it's time to close the store. I'll…ah… go do that, and you two do…whatever it is you're doing."

The instant Haley left them alone, Cole quit playing around. This was serious. This was his chance, and no way in hell was he going to screw it up again.

For the second time that day, he walked over to Rachel and cradled her face in his hands, tipped her head so that their gazes met. "I shouldn't have pretended to love another woman, sweetheart. But if doing so brought you here tonight, then I would do it again. Without hesitation or so much as a second thought."

"Is that so?" she asked in an almost breathless voice.

"Yes, that's so. And I hope you've already figured out that what I said about Mary, about not being able to move on with her, wasn't true. I didn't know you knew," he said with a grimace. "I'm sorry if I hurt you with those words."

Relief swept into her gaze, her expression. "So, what you're saying is that you can move on with…Mary?"

"Yes, sweetheart. Though I really do prefer the name Cupcake." He paused then, to add weight to these next vital words. This was it. Everything he'd wanted, right here. "I love you, Rachel Merriday. I have loved you for so long, that I don't recall when I didn't."

"Aw, you're so sweet," she said after a beat. She smiled, paused for second. Two. Three. Hell, he needed to hear the words. Needed her to say she loved him, too. Then, with a bat of her eyelashes, said, "Thank you, so very much."

He blinked once. Twice. Three times. "Thank…you?"

"My mother taught me to give gratitude when someone says something nice." Rachel looked at him with the straightest darn face he'd ever seen. With the slightest of shrugs, she said, "You said something nice. So…thank you, Cole. From the bottom of my heart."

Well, hell. What was a man supposed to do with that? "Uh. You're welcome?"

"I." Standing up on her tiptoes, she brushed her lips on his neck. "Love." Then across his jaw. "You." To his ear. "Too." And then, finally and blessedly, to his mouth. "But I can do one better than you, mister. I'll love you forever, I will never stop. And that…well, that's simply a fact."

Their lips met. Her mouth opened and the tiniest of moans slipped from her throat. Need and desire roared to life in his blood, in his body, in every cell, and in every nerve. Only for Rachel had he ever felt like this. Only for Rachel would he ever feel like this.

He feathered his fingers into her hair and pushed her head closer, kissing her fully, reveling in the passion that existed between them. It was, at once, hungry and satiating, longing and fulfilling, unique and…familiar. This was Rachel, the woman he loved.

The woman who loved him. His Cupcake.

Epilogue

Snuggling up to Cole's warm, sleeping body, Rachel sighed in absolute, to her toes, blissful contentment. Had she ever been this happy? She didn't have to consider the question for long to find the answer. No, she had not ever, in her entire life, been this happy.

Or satisfied, for that matter.

Friday night, after they'd finally put the past to rest, they'd returned to Rachel's house. When Cole had seen the bare tree lying at the side of the curb, he'd insisted on hauling it back in. If no other reason existed, that little action right there would have stolen Rachel's heart.

Cole had popped popcorn and made hot chocolate, stating that those were the official snack foods for the Christmas tree decorating season, and then together, they'd restrung the lights and rehung the ornaments, laughing and teasing and kissing as they did.

The evening had been filled with Christmas magic.

The rest of the night had been filled with an altogether different type of magic, one of a much steamier variety.

Oh, yes, Rachel considered herself a very happy and satisfied woman.

She stroked her hand down Cole's bare hip, rose up on her other elbow so she could see the clock. Fifteen more minutes until Christmas. Fifteen more excruciating minutes.

Darn if she didn't feel as if she were a six-year-old little girl, waiting impatiently for Santa to arrive. This year, though, she wasn't interested in dolls or games—definitely no games, please—or storybooks. This year, she had her heart set on one very particular, very glittery gift.

She fidgeted again, rolled over to peek at the clock again, saw that an entire sixty seconds had passed since she'd last checked and groaned loudly. Watched Cole to see if he budged. That would be a no. Hmm. She was sure, with some minor creativity, she could wake him up.

But then, they wouldn't get to the presents until well after midnight.

"You are the most impatient woman I have ever met," Cole said, his voice thick with sleep and humor. "I believe the rule was no presents until eight in the morning."

"Um. You were serious about that?" She'd thought he was teasing her. "Because if so, Cole Foster, that is entirely unfair. Why, Christmas is official in—" she propped herself up again to look "—twelve minutes."

"We'll wait until morning," he said stubbornly. "That's the Foster rule."

"I am not a Foster," she said. Yet. Or so she hoped.

He lazily moved his hand to her breast and trailed his finger around her nipple. Delicious heat rippled through her abdomen. He laughed a slow, lazy chuckle, saying,

"You already know what all of your gifts are, so why are you in such a rush?"

She sniffed, donned a faux-sarcastic voice and said, "Well, I didn't know they were for me when we bought them, did I? Or half of them, anyway."

"You just want those tattoos, admit it."

And the poodle. Oh, and she couldn't wait to find out why he deemed a flashlight romantic. The stubborn man had refused to give her an explanation, stating she needed at least one surprise for Christmas morning. She was hoping for two.

"I'm more excited about the T-shirt," she teased.

Rolling onto his side, he faced her. His other hand flattened on her stomach, eliciting another delicious curl of heat. "You aren't really going to make me get up and open gifts at midnight, are you? That's just...cruel."

"Yes, I think I am." There was just enough light in the room for her to make out the strong features of his face. She wondered, briefly, who their someday children would take after in looks. She hoped for a brood of tough little boys with coal-black hair and chocolate-brown eyes. "I love you," she whispered. "So very much."

"I love you, too." Gripping her hips, he dragged her closer to him and kissed her softly on the mouth. "You've made me the happiest man in the world, darlin'."

She grinned. "Thank you."

He growled and kissed her again. Harder this time. Demanding and hot, searching and hungry. She moaned and ran her hands down his bare, muscular back, enjoying the feel of his warm skin, savoring the sensations of their bodies touching.

He moved his mouth to her neck, down to her shoulder blade and then to her breast, where his tongue swirled, creating more heat, more desire, more everything to tumble through Rachel's body. "I want you," he groaned. "Again. Now."

His words, his tenor, the heat in his voice made her tremble, shiver, with her own want, her own very real need for this man. Her man. "That is a very good idea. And," she said, glancing at the clock, "we still have eight minutes."

"Eight minutes, huh?" His eyes locked with hers, and even in the dim glow, she could easily read his amusement mixed in with his hunger. "Now, darlin', I'm not quite sure—"

"Shut up and kiss me," she demanded. "The clock is ticking."

His mouth returned to hers and she melted into the kiss, into him. Rachel forgot all about Christmas and the gifts waiting downstairs. Simply speaking, the world ceased to exist for a very long time. Considerably more than eight minutes.

It was, in fact, dawn by the time they made it downstairs.

Now, they were sitting in front of the newly decorated Christmas tree. A pile of presents—ten of them to be exact—were heaped next to Rachel's feet. Cole had already opened the solitary present Rachel had given him—the midnight-blue nightgown she'd modeled with such delight in the dressing room—and from the look in his eyes, he was ready to drag her back upstairs. She was good with that. Really, really, really good.

But not until she opened her presents.

"I'm sorry I don't have more gifts for you," she said, somewhat embarrassed. Her first romantic Christmas with Cole, and she'd been so wrapped up in the glory of him—of them—that yes, she'd totally spaced off shopping. She'd make it up to him next Christmas.

And every day in between now and then.

"I believe I have everything I've ever wished for this Christmas, Rach." He paused, reached over and ran his thumb over her lips. "You. You're the only gift I wanted this year."

She blinked as emotion welled within. Yes. Every day between now and next Christmas…and beyond. "Well, maybe later, I'll put that on—" she directed her gaze toward the box with the nightgown "—along with some strategically placed Christmas bows, and see to it that a few more of your…wishes come true."

"Open your gifts," he said in that growling way of his. "Before I take you up on that."

Staring at him, at Cole, for one more minute, she allowed the warmth and contentment to swell within her. Important elements of a relationship, yes. But also, with Cole, was this absolute surety that he was exactly the right man for her. And yes, that she was exactly the right woman for him. What a joyous gift to have, to be.

She was a very fortunate woman. On both accounts.

"Come on, Rach," Cole said, waking her from her thoughts. "Open your gifts."

Nodding, she focused on the presents. She could tell by their sizes and shapes which was which, and yes, there were precisely ten. For the moment, she wouldn't let that concern her. Cole might have slid the ring into any one of these other gifts, or he might be saving it for last.

She decided to start with the silly gifts, the ones they'd chosen after she'd discovered the charade. None of those needed an explanation, after all. The tattoos were first, then the shirt, then the chocolates—she would never eat all of those chocolates—and then the toy poodle.

Holding it up, she pressed the poodle's stomach and

a "Yip, yip, yip" erupted. "This," Rachel said to Cole, "is Cupcake. So, if you refer to 'Cupcake' in any way, shape or form, I will assume you want this." She grinned and tossed the stuffed animal at him.

He caught it and made the thing yip again. "Actually, no. You are my Cupcake. This is…um…we'll go with Cocoa. Yeah, I like that."

"Brat," she said, before reaching for and opening the red negligee.

"And when you wear that," Cole added with a wicked gleam in his eyes, "I'll call you Jezebel…or maybe Bambi. Both would work, don't you think?"

She wrinkled her nose and threw the flimsy piece of silk at him, as well, before appraising the remaining gifts. Probably, the photo album—if Cole had, indeed, filled it with pictures of them—would make her cry. The flashlight, depending on his reason for purchasing it, might also pack an emotional punch. She'd save those for last.

After opening the small bottle of perfume, Rachel spritzed it on her wrists and behind her ears. "This one really ticked me off, by the way," she said. "The thought of you loving some other woman was bad enough. The thought of her wearing my scent around you?"

"Didn't like that, huh?"

"Uh. That would be a no." Moving on, Rachel selected the snow globe next, and she and Cole spent a few minutes reminiscing about the day they'd met.

It was, she decided, very fortuitous that her gaze had landed on Cole and his brothers before any of the other groups of children. One look at them whizzing snowballs at each other had resulted in the desperate longing to join them.

Yes, very fortuitous.

The camera required zero discussion, so she set the gift aside with the idea she'd snap pictures of Cole and his family later that day. Hmm. Photo album or flashlight?

She had to go for the flashlight. The big, honking flashlight that would easily light up an entire room. "Okay. I have to know," she said, holding the flashlight by its handle and waving it in front of her. Ha. It was heavy enough so that she could use it to exercise with. "Why is this romantic?"

"That's easy," Cole said, leaning toward her and removing the flashlight from her grasp. "I don't like the idea of you driving alone at night. This flashlight offers the practical use it's intended for, but also…well, if you were to run into trouble, it's heavy, so you can use it to bash some guy over his head, giving you long enough to run away and call for help."

Rachel blinked, taking this in. Yeah, that was romantic. Her heart softened and swelled. He wanted to protect her, even when she wasn't with him. She shook her head, laughing, loving the way his brain worked. "Practical and romantic. I see it now. Thank you."

His voice turned gruff when he said, "Welcome. I always want you to be safe."

And with him, she was sure she would be. He'd see to it.

The last gift, the one that Rachel was certain would bring tears flowing from her eyes, remained. Reaching for the wrapped package, she picked it up and peeled off the tape slowly, and then the paper, trying to prepare herself for whatever photos Cole had included as part of "their journey so far." An incredible journey, fraught with ups and downs.

When the last bit of paper was removed, she stared

at the closed album for a few seconds, and then slowly opened the first page. "Oh," she said, smiling. There they were, a young Cole and a younger Rachel, sitting on his parents' front porch. "I remember that day. Your mom made us shovel the driveway because we were driving her batty in the house."

"Yup. Keep looking, Rach," Cole said, his voice warm, holding a nuance of anticipation.

One by one, she flipped the pages, seeing herself and Cole grow up before her eyes. Boating in the summer. Sledding in the winter. Grouped in front of the Fosters' Christmas tree with Cole's brothers and sister. Building snowmen and snow forts.

Year by year, picture by picture, her entire relationship with Cole was represented. It was, Rachel reflected, the sweetest, most thoughtful, most romantic gift she'd ever received.

The last page that held pictures—he'd left several pages open for them to fill with new photos—was from the prior Christmas. One of them, a photo Rachel hadn't seen before, was of the two of them sitting next to each other at a table at Foster's. She remembered this moment, as well. Vividly, in fact.

Cole's mother had taken the photo. Rachel was leaning against Cole, his arm was wrapped over her shoulders, and they were looking at each other, rather than at the camera.

She'd been leaving that day, Rachel remembered, disappointed that the visit hadn't turned out the way she'd hoped. Hell. *Disappointed* wasn't the right word. She'd been devastated. And now, she knew he'd been the feeling the same.

"We lost so much time," she whispered. "So much time we could have spent together."

"I know," Cole said, his voice heavy with every emotion Rachel was experiencing. "But sweetheart, those days make up our past. They're part of who we are now. And I don't know about you, but it's because of that past…because of the time lost, that I know I will count my blessings every single day from here on out. No more lost time. Not for us."

With those very intelligent words, Rachel let go of her regret. She closed the photo album and leaned her head against Cole's shoulder. "You're right," she said. "No more lost time. I like the sound of that. Very, very much."

They kissed, deeply and passionately. Then, Cole whispered in her ear, "We have a few hours before going to my parents. Feel like modeling that gown for me again? Upstairs?"

Okay, so there wouldn't be a ring. There wouldn't be a proposal. Rachel put away her disappointment. What was important, what mattered, was that she and Cole were together. She loved him. He loved her. Maybe next Christmas. Or the one after. Or, the one after that. Whenever he was ready to ask, she was ready to say yes.

Until then, she'd enjoy…well, them.

"Yes, please," she said. "First, though, let me go find those Christmas bows."

The Foster house was packed with more people than Rachel had ever seen within its walls. In addition to the six Fosters she knew and loved, there were an additional ten in residence. Paul Foster's brother's family and their families were here from Portland, Oregon, celebrating the holidays.

She'd been introduced to everyone: John and his wife, Karen, their three sons and their families, which included Grady, his wife, Olivia, and their adorably cute four-month-old son, Levi; Jace and his wife, Melanie; and finally, Seth, his fiancée, Rebecca, and their beyond beautiful five-month-old daughter, Grace.

Everyone was very nice and very excited to be in Colorado for Christmas. Over dinner, Rachel had learned a little about each of the couples, and could honestly say she liked them all. She probably had the most in common with Olivia, as they'd had similar upbringings, but she found Melanie and Rebecca to be lovely, interesting and intelligent women.

Frankly, if they lived closer together, she was fairly sure she'd become close friends with all three of the women. It was the men, though, that really took Rachel's breath away. Holy cow, the Foster genes created some seriously sexy men.

Heck, it was obvious they were all related. All tall, all with the same lean, muscular builds, and for five of the six, the same shade of hair and eyes. Which was a little odd, seeing how Paul's brother had vivid blue, not brown, eyes, but she figured the brown was just hiding in the Oregon patriarch's DNA.

And even Dylan, with his lighter hair and green eyes, resembled the others enough that there was no mistaking him for anything but a Foster. Well, Haley, too, for that matter.

Rachel sighed and sat down in the nearest empty chair. Sinful, really, how one family had produced so many beautiful, sexy offspring.

"You look overwhelmed," said Olivia, taking the chair next to her. She had an almost-asleep Levi cradled against her shoulder. "We can be a lot, until you get to know us all."

"Oh, I'm not overwhelmed at all. I'm just—" Rachel shrugged "—really happy."

"Christmas is a good day for happy." Olivia smiled as one of Levi's plump fists came up to grab a chunk of her long, dark hair. "He likes having something to hold on to when he's falling asleep," she explained. "If I'm holding him, it's my hair. If Grady is, it's his shirt."

Everything inside Rachel softened as she looked at the baby. "He's just gorgeous."

Olivia's smile widened. "Thank you. We think so."

Soon, Melanie joined them, complaining—though Rachel didn't think she was all that serious, due to the sparkle in her light brown eyes—about how her husband, Jace, had just lost her a game of Uno by announcing all the cards she'd had in her hand.

Rachel laughed. "What? Why did he do that?"

"Oh, he didn't mean to. He was trying to advise me on strategy." She shook her head and tossed an indulgent look toward the man in question, who was ambling toward them. "Because he believes he's the Uno king."

Jace plopped himself down on the arm of Melanie's chair. "I am the Uno king. And if you'd just listened to me, you could've won that game."

The two fell into a bit of friendly squabbling. In another few minutes, Seth and Rebecca pulled two other chairs up to the group, and then Dylan, Reid and Haley—holding baby Grace, who was also asleep—did the same. And Rachel could not have been happier.

This was family. Right here. God, she loved it.

Everyone chatted about this and that. She tried to keep up with the various topics, laughed here and there, but for the most part, remained quiet and…happy.

After a while, she started missing her Foster man. She glanced around, looking for him. Nope. Not one Cole Foster to be seen. Maybe he was in the kitchen. She started to rise to a stand, intent on locating him, when Jace tugged her arm hard enough she fell back into her chair.

"Where are you going, Rachel?" he asked with a friendly grin. "Can't leave now, not when we're talking about…uh—" he glanced at his wife "—what were we talking about?"

"You're a dork," she said half under her breath. "We were just saying how much we loved skiing the other day. It really is beautiful here!"

"Yes, beautiful!" chimed Olivia. Then, seeing her husband, she said, "Grady, come here and tell Rachel how much we're loving our trip so far."

Ah. They seemed a little too enthusiastic. She glanced at Reid, hoping he might offer some illumination, but all he did was shrug and smile. And Dylan was too busy tugging on his sister's hair to be of any help.

"Actually, I just wanted to find Cole," Rachel said, trying to stand again.

Jace pulled her down. Again. "Uh. You can't. You have to sit here," he said with a spark of desperation. "We just met you. We'll be going back to Oregon in a few days, so—"

"What my simple-headed husband is trying to say," Melanie said, elbowing Jace in his side, "is we won't have much time to get to know you. Who knows when we'll be out here again?"

"Just stay," Haley inserted. "Talk to us for a while."

Seth and Rebecca murmured similar sentiments.

Grady strolled over, grinned at Rachel. "Is my brother picking on you?"

Rachel blinked. This was becoming beyond odd. "A little. Do you know where Cole is?"

"Oh, he'll be out here momentarily, I believe," Grady said, moving to stand behind Olivia's chair. He rested his hand on his son's head. "No reason to go in search of him."

And then, all at once, the remaining Fosters—minus Cole—streamed into the already crowded room, finding spots to sit or stand in. She glanced around again, saw that everyone was either looking at her or toward the other end of the room, and she knew that something was up.

And unless Rachel was mistaken, Cole was at the center of it.

"What's going on?" she asked, focusing on Margaret Foster. Cole's mom smiled sweetly in return, but didn't offer an explanation.

"You'll see," Haley said, which earned her a smack on the back of her head from Dylan.

"They're waiting for me to give you this," Cole said, his deep voice entering the fray. "And they've been darn impatient about it. Family," he said with a grin, "can drive a man nuts."

Rachel's heart went to her throat. She whipped her vision to him. He was carrying a large, rectangular box—far too big to be a ring box—and was coming toward her with that sexy smile she adored. "We already exchanged presents," she said, stating the obvious.

"I had one more for you, but it was here for safekeeping." He placed the box in front of her, looked for a place to sit and finding none, said, "Geez, guys. Thanks for saving me a chair."

"You're young enough to sit on the floor and still be able to stand up," his father said.

Cole shrugged, grinned at Rachel and dropped to the floor. "Go on, Rach. Open the present. This is the one I've been waiting all day to give you. And," he said with a wink, "you don't know what this gift is, because you weren't with me when I bought it."

Well, doh. Even though Rachel knew this was not what it first seemed, her heart pounded in her chest fast and hard, and goose bumps were sprouting on her arms.

With a shaking hand, she started to pick off the tape on the corner of the box. Various members of the Foster families called out for her to "just rip the paper off," so with a last questioning look at Cole, who nodded his agreement, she did.

She tore a long sheet right from the front of the box, blinked, shook her head and blinked again, staring in disbelief. "Really, Cole?" Laughter burbled in her throat. What was she going to do with this man? "A vacuum cleaner. You bought me a freaking vacuum cleaner?"

"Rachel," he said, his voice urgent and intense. "Look at me."

The trembling grew stronger. The shivers increased. Her goose bumps spread to every inch of her body. She looked.

Cole was on one knee holding a small, black velvet jewelry box in his hand. With his other, he shoved the vacuum cleaner out of the way. "Rachel," he said again, his eyes meeting and holding hers, "will you do me the honor of—" the very air in the room seemed to still in anticipation "—vacuuming my rugs for…the rest of our lives?"

The tears started then. She didn't care, didn't try to stop them. They rolled down her cheeks, dripping off her chin. "Idiot," she whispered, her voice shaking. "You just had to go and prove to me that even a vacuum cleaner can be a romantic gift, didn't you?"

"Did I?"

"Oh, yes."

"And will you?" he asked. "You haven't answered my first question yet."

She wasn't letting him get off that easy. "Will I... what?"

"Will you, Rachel Merriday, marry me?"

"Yes. I will marry you, Cole Foster." She blinked to clear her vision, which immediately filled with fresh tears. He reached for her left hand, grasped her wrist. Oh, wow. This was really happening. But, "Let me make one thing clear—you'll do all the vacuuming in our home."

He didn't respond, just opened the jeweler's box. And there...there it was, the beautiful, perfect ring she'd been dreaming of ever since she'd seen it on her finger before. That had only been temporary, though. Nothing but pretend.

Sliding the exquisite ring on her finger, Cole let out a deep, satisfied breath. "There. Now my Christmas wish has come true."

And this...well, this was delightfully, wonderfully, beautifully real.

The entire room of Fosters burst into cheers, offering congratulations and laughter.

"This is forever," Rachel said. "And that's a—"

"Fact," Cole said before drawing her into his arms for a long, lusty kiss.

Yes, Rachel thought, this was forever. She would love this man every single minute of every single day for the rest of her life. Forever friends.

And thankfully, so much more than that.

* * * * *

REQUEST YOUR FREE BOOKS!

2 FREE NOVELS PLUS 2 FREE GIFTS!

✦ Harlequin®

SPECIAL EDITION

Life, Love & Family

YES! Please send me 2 FREE Harlequin® Special Edition novels and my 2 FREE gifts (gifts are worth about $10). After receiving them, if I don't wish to receive any more books, I can return the shipping statement marked "cancel." If I don't cancel, I will receive 6 brand-new novels every month and be billed just $4.49 per book in the U.S. or $5.24 per book in Canada. That's a saving of at least 14% off the cover price! It's quite a bargain! Shipping and handling is just 50¢ per book in the U.S. and 75¢ per book in Canada.* I understand that accepting the 2 free books and gifts places me under no obligation to buy anything. I can always return a shipment and cancel at any time. Even if I never buy another book, the two free books and gifts are mine to keep forever.

235/335 HDN FEGF

Name _____ (PLEASE PRINT)

Address _____ Apt. #

City _____ State/Prov. _____ Zip/Postal Code

Signature (if under 18, a parent or guardian must sign)

Mail to the **Reader Service:**
IN U.S.A.: P.O. Box 1867, Buffalo, NY 14240-1867
IN CANADA: P.O. Box 609, Fort Erie, Ontario L2A 5X3

Not valid for current subscribers to Harlequin Special Edition books.

Want to try two free books from another line?
Call 1-800-873-8635 or visit www.ReaderService.com.

* Terms and prices subject to change without notice. Prices do not include applicable taxes. Sales tax applicable in N.Y. Canadian residents will be charged applicable taxes. Offer not valid in Quebec. This offer is limited to one order per household. All orders subject to credit approval. Credit or debit balances in a customer's account(s) may be offset by any other outstanding balance owed by or to the customer. Please allow 4 to 6 weeks for delivery. Offer available while quantities last.

Your Privacy—The Reader Service is committed to protecting your privacy. Our Privacy Policy is available online at www.ReaderService.com or upon request from the Reader Service.

We make a portion of our mailing list available to reputable third parties that offer products we believe may interest you. If you prefer that we not exchange your name with third parties, or if you wish to clarify or modify your communication preferences, please visit us at www.ReaderService.com/consumerschoice or write to us at Reader Service Preference Service, P.O. Box 9062, Buffalo, NY 14269. Include your complete name and address.

HSE11B

Turn the page for a preview of

THE OTHER SIDE OF US

by

Sarah Mayberry,

*coming January 2013
from Harlequin® Superromance®.*

*PLUS, exciting changes are in the works!
Enjoy the same great stories in a longer format
and new look—beginning January 2013!*

THE OTHER SIDE OF US
A brand-new novel
from Harlequin® Superromance® author
Sarah Mayberry

In recovery from a serious accident, Mackenzie Williams
is beating all the doctors' predictions. But she needs
single-minded focus. She doesn't *need the distraction*
of neighbors—especially good-looking ones
like Oliver Garrett!

MACKENZIE BREATHED DEEPLY to recover from the workout. She'd pushed herself too far but she wanted to accelerate her rehabilitation. Still, she needed to lie down to combat the nausea and shaking muscles.

There was a knock on the front door. Who on earth would be visiting her on a Thursday morning? Probably a cold-calling salesperson.

She answered, but her pithy rejection died before she'd formed the first words.

The man on her doorstep was definitely not a cold caller. Nothing about this man was cold, from the auburn of his wavy hair to his brown eyes to his sensual mouth. Nothing cold about those broad shoulders, flat belly and lean hips, either.

"Hey," he said in a shiver-inducing baritone. "I'm Oliver Garrett. I moved in next door." His smile was so warm and vibrant it was almost offensive.

"Mackenzie Williams." Oh, no. Her legs were starting to

tremble, indicating they wouldn't hold up long. Any second now she would embarrass herself in front of this complete and very good-looking stranger.

"It's been years since I was down here." He seemed to settle in for a chat. "It doesn't look as though—"

"I have to go." Her stomach rolled as she shut the door. The last thing she registered was the look of shock on Oliver's face at her abrupt dismissal.

And somehow she knew their neighborly relations would be a lot cooler now.

Will Mackenzie be able to make it up to Oliver for her rude introduction?
Find out in THE OTHER SIDE OF US
by Sarah Mayberry, available January 2013 from Harlequin® Superromance®. PLUS, exciting changes are in the works! Enjoy the same great stories in a longer format and new look—beginning January 2013!